WITCH UNDERCOVER

A BLAIR WILKES MYSTERY

ELLE ADAMS

This book was written, produced and edited in the UK, where some spelling, grammar and word usage will vary from US English.

Copyright © 2018 Elle Adams
All rights reserved.

To be notified when Elle Adams's next book is released, sign up to her author newsletter.

1

"Miaow," said Sky.

The little cat padded ahead of Nathan and me, downhill towards the lake. Towards home.

Home. The first time I'd stumbled into the town of Fairy Falls, I certainly hadn't thought I'd ever think of it as my home. But after a week away, the sight of the cluster of buildings by the lake brought a rush of emotion welling within me.

The chill winter air bit at my exposed skin as I walked downhill. Nathan's walking boots were designed for trekking through the hills, but my own boots would have been submerged if I hadn't activated their levitation mode. Seven Millimetre boots—a downgraded version of the Seven League boots which had once been popular throughout the magical world—could step seven millimetres at a time in any direction, including off the ground. I got on much better with my own form of transport than I did riding a broomstick, and as a bonus, the boots made it easier to keep up with Nathan's long-legged stride.

As we drew closer to town, doubts began to creep in. We'd been away for a nice holiday by the sea, but I'd also travelled with another purpose: to translate the mysterious letter my jailed father had sent me on the solstice. Since the note had been written in a code I couldn't read, I'd had to ask a specialist, but even though I'd had the translation in hand for days, I had yet to read the words of the note. Dad hadn't been in a hurry for me to read it, given its cryptic nature, but the longer I waited, the harder it became to take the plunge. Now I was almost out of excuses. I'd be back at work tomorrow in the office of Dritch & Co, the paranormal recruitment company which had brought me into the magical world, and I'd also be starting the next round of my magical education. My best bet was to get it over with before life got hectic again.

The winding cobbled streets of Fairy Falls had become more familiar to me than anywhere else, from the neat houses by the lake to the more modern structure of the new jail. Nathan halted outside the police station next door. Inside, I could see several of the gargoyles who ran the town's police force milling around. I'd bet Steve hadn't let them take the holidays off.

"I have to go," said Nathan. "I need to report to Steve, who'll have a ton of paperwork saved up for my return, I don't doubt."

I frowned at the police station. "You're supposed to be on holiday."

"I'll make sure he doesn't put me on the night shift." He pulled me into a hug. "Promise."

"I'll hold you to that." I wrapped my arms around him

and kissed him. "Let me know if your sister's back in town. I have words to say to her fiancé."

Nathan's sister, Erin, had just moved to Fairy Falls herself. Her arrival had caused a stir, mostly thanks to her fiancé—who, the last time I'd seen him, had been an active paranormal hunter. Like Erin herself had used to be, along with Nathan and their entire family.

As well as a paranormal hunter, Buck also happened to be the only other half-fairy I'd met in the paranormal world. After months of believing I was one of a kind, I had no end of questions I wanted to ask him. But right now, it was time to go home… and tell Alissa the truth.

Worry squirmed within me at the thought. Alissa was my best friend, but because she was dating a vampire librarian who could read minds, anything I told her in confidence might end up spreading around the town's entire vampire population even if she didn't tell another soul. I'd been avoiding the vampires for weeks, too, given the number of secrets wriggling around inside my head, but I knew better than to think I could keep such a major secret from my best friend indefinitely.

My heels dragged on the pavement as I made my way to the large, grand house where I shared a flat with Alissa. She was the granddaughter of Madame Grey, the town's leader, who'd welcomed me into Fairy Falls despite my family's slightly unconventional history.

Really, it was a wonder I'd found my way to the magical world at all. As I'd been adopted by ordinary humans, I'd had no idea that my mother, Tanith Wild-flower, had once lived here in Fairy Falls, before she'd fallen in love with a fairy and ran away from her coven. The next time she'd been heard of, she'd been on the run from the paranormal hunters and had died before they could jail her. As for my dad, he was currently serving a lifetime sentence in the Lancashire Prison for Paranormals—the most secure magical prison in the region, reserved for the worst of criminals.

While most people believed the prison's inhabitants to be guilty beyond all doubt, I'd spoken to my mother's ghost a couple of months ago and confirmed that she'd committed the crime of stealing the Head Witch's sceptre in order to protect her family. I knew she was no criminal, and my dad wasn't either. Unfortunately, that opinion wasn't shared by the paranormal hunters—including the Inquisitor, the owner of the prison and the reason my dad had worried about his letters being intercepted.

The Inquisitor, who was a fairy, like me.

I'd only guessed the truth recently, but while I'd told Nathan, there was little either of us could do about it. Even Madame Grey couldn't stand up to the hunters. They'd deemed my dad guilty, and that was that. But despite it all, he'd found a way to send a letter to me, and soon the truth would be in my hands. One way or another.

"Should I open the note, Sky?" I asked my cat.

"Miaow," he said, which probably meant *hurry up*. I'd dawdled enough, so I quickened my pace towards home.

I unlocked the front door to the large house and entered the hallway, where the door on my right led into the flat which I shared with Alissa. I unlocked that, too, and Sky sidled his way through ahead of me.

Our cosy-sized flat contained a living room laid out with plain but functional wooden furniture, a bookshelf stacked with magical textbooks—most on healing, since

Alissa worked at the local hospital—and a comfy sofa and armchairs. Alissa sat on the sofa reading a book. Roald, her cat, raised his head as Sky came into the room.

"Blair!" Alissa leapt up and ran to hug me. "I didn't know you were back in town."

"Nathan had to go and report to Steve," I explained. "The old gargoyle will be laying on the guilt, I don't doubt, depending on how many crimes have taken place since we left."

"Nothing major." She gave me a grin. "It's been positively quiet without you here."

"Ha," I said. "In fairness, it's Christmas. Maybe even paranormal criminals take the holidays off."

"Maybe," she said. "There were a few incidents at New Year's parties, but not enough to warrant the whole security force being sent out."

"Well, I've arrived in time to bring a new wave of chaos for the new year." I carried my suitcase through the door to my bedroom and left it with my rucksack to unpack later. If I started now, I'd end up using it as an excuse to put off opening my dad's note.

"Miaow." Sky picked up the note in his mouth and shoved it into my hands. If *that* wasn't a clear message, I didn't know what was, so I took the note with me, along with the other slip of paper which contained the translation.

Alissa waited for me in the kitchen, making tea. "So, how was your holiday?"

"Great," I answered. "I mean, the weather wasn't amazing, but it's been nice to see more of the paranormal world and get away from the chaos for a bit."

I'd have been happy to avoid the paranormal hunters

for the foreseeable future, too. After all, the Inquisitor had tried to hire me to join the hunters myself, which had made no sense to me, given my family history. But his words took on a whole new meaning now I knew we were both fairies. I'd need to ask my dad about it… depending on what he'd said in his note.

Alissa finished making the tea and carried the two mugs to the sofa. Already, Sky had made himself at home by stealing Roald's spot. I sat down slowly, the two pieces of paper clenched in my hand.

"You wanted to tell me something before you left," she said. "Right?"

Where to begin? "So… my dad left me this note." I held up the papers. "But this time, he decided to be extra cautious and write it in some kind of fairy code. I had to take it with me to a specialist who worked at a magical library to figure out the translation."

Her eyes rounded. "So that's why you picked a town with a magical library."

"One of the reasons," I said. "I didn't know if it'd work, but it looks like it did. I haven't read it yet."

Alissa sipped her tea. "Why not?"

"It's like Schrodinger's Cat," I said. "As long as I don't open the note, it can't be good news *or* bad news."

"Miaow," Sky said, which probably meant, *hey, keep me out of it.*

"I'm sure it's not bad news," she said. "He meant you to take the time to find out its translation, too. You hadn't heard from him in a while, either."

"No, but there's a good reason for that."

Since my dad had been jailed long before I'd entered the paranormal world, our only means of communication had been for him to send a pixie to deliver notes. Now I knew the man who owned the jail was a fairy himself, it became clear how big a risk he'd taken in keeping the lines of communication open.

I sucked in a deep breath and unfolded the note. The first line said, *I'm sorry I couldn't see you, Blair.*

A few lines followed that I couldn't read, not without the translation.

Then I turned to the second page and read on.

I tried to keep you out of this world. I should have known there was too much of your mother in you.

My lungs constricted. It was suddenly hard to breathe.

"Blair?" Alissa peered at me. "You okay?"

I nodded mutely and read on. *If you wish to stay in this world, then there are things you must know. I do not know how much you've heard about the reasons for my imprisonment, but there is such a thing as a Pixie-Glass that will enable us to talk directly. If you find one, I will tell you how to use it, but I cannot share any more in this form of communication.*

You might want to start with the market.

I lowered the note, my insides churning. "Have you ever heard of a Pixie-Glass?"

"A what?" said Alissa. "Pixie-Glass? No, why?"

"My dad says it can help us communicate with one another so he can tell me why he was jailed," I said. "I *knew* he was innocent. The Inquisitor has him under close watch, so he can't say anything more direct in a note, not even written in code."

"Blair…" She paused. "Not that I don't want you to be able to speak to your dad, but the Inquisitor is *the* head of all magical authority in the region. And he already knows who you are."

"He wants to recruit me," I added. "Or he did, before I turned him down. I'll talk to Nathan and see what we can do, but it's worth looking into what this Pixie-Glass might be. The note says to start with the market. What kind of market?"

Her brow wrinkled. "No idea. Some magical towns have a market, but this one doesn't."

"Yeah... I know." Yet another mystery. Knowing how much danger my dad's messages might put me in didn't quite banish my frustration at the hoops I had to jump through just to figure out what he wanted to say to me. And he *was* innocent, I was certain. Like my mother, he'd got on the hunters' bad side and paid the price for it.

"By the way," Alissa said, "someone sent a message for you while you were gone."

I looked up. "Not my dad?"

"No... it came from the normal world." She held up an envelope covered in stamps and scribbled addresses which were incomprehensible to me.

"What the...?" I turned the envelope over and opened it, pulling out a slip of folded paper. Unfolding it, I found a note from my foster parents, addressed from somewhere in Australia. *Blair, please call us as soon as possible.*

I lowered my hands, my heart jerking into a fast beat. "My foster parents. How did they even find me here?"

Judging by the confusing mass of scribbles on the envelope, they'd originally sent the letter to my former address back in the normal world, but nobody at that address would have known whereabouts I'd moved to. Yet through some magical intervention, the letter had somehow found its way to me here in Fairy Falls.

"They could have texted you, right?" said Alissa. "Or called."

"Maybe they can't." My heartbeat quickened even further. "Maybe it's urgent. It has to be."

Combined with my dad's note, my worries multiplied tenfold. My hands shook as I pulled out my mobile phone and called my foster mum's number.

"Hello?" I said as soon as someone picked up. "It's me."

"Blair!" said Mrs Wilkes. "We're back."

"Back?" I frowned.

"Yes, it was a *long* flight, but we're back in England," she said. "It's bloody freezing, isn't it?"

Oh. Oh, no. I'd forgotten my foster parents had planned to return from their long trip to Australia by Christmas. "Uh, I only just got your letter. When did you send it, a month ago?"

"I thought it'd take a while to reach you," she said cheerily. "We're at home now and still unpacking everything, but I'd love to see you."

My throat tightened. I hadn't wanted to cut my family out of my life, but sharing the paranormal world with outsiders wasn't allowed. No exceptions.

"We just have to meet your boyfriend," added Mrs Wilkes. "And see that wonderful new home of yours. It sounds like you've been having a great time."

Oh. God. What was I supposed to do? "Um, I actually just got back from a holiday with my boyfriend. Five minutes ago. That's why it took me so long to get your letter and call you back. And I start back at work tomorrow, so I need to check my calendar and..."

Mrs Wilkes cut through my babbling. "Don't worry,

just give me a call when you know your schedule. It's great being back in the same country as you!"

"I know,' I said weakly. "I'll see what I can do."

It seemed my biological family weren't the only relatives I had to worry about.

2

The following morning, I slept in late, and would have missed my alarm altogether if Sky hadn't jabbed his claws into my leg and then climbed on my face.

It was entirely my own fault, because I'd been awake half the night trying to figure out how to bring my foster parents into my new life without actually inviting them into Fairy Falls itself. So far, I'd drawn a total blank. While they didn't necessarily have to come to my house, I couldn't hide the town's magical nature from them unless I gave a decently convincing reason why they couldn't come and visit. Or invented an entirely new town, which was pretty much what I'd already been doing over the phone—but it was a lot easier to bluff when we were ten thousand miles apart. Now they were home, I'd need to come up with an ironclad cover story and then stick to it.

At the moment, though, I couldn't even find my work clothes. I ran around the flat, searched my suitcase, and was about to call Nathan and ask him whether I'd left them at his house when I spotted a sleeve poking out from under the bed.

"Really, Sky?" I crouched down to find my entire collection of work clothes lying in a heap on the carpet. Apparently, my cat had been busy last night. "You couldn't have left me one outfit?"

In answer, Sky pretended to be asleep.

I retrieved my clothes—every item now covered in cat hair—and hurried to dress for work. Perhaps Sky resented no longer being on holiday, but he was the one who got to sleep all day, while I didn't even have time to grab a coffee before running along to work.

I approached Dritch & Co's office with some trepidation, but Veronica wasn't in the reception area waiting to chastise me for being late. Callie, the blond receptionist, gave me a cheery wave as I walked in.

"Glad to see you're back, Blair."

"Same here." Despite the occasional troublesome client, working at Dritch & Co was the best job I'd had in my adult life—and the longest I'd lasted in any position, come to that. "Is the boss around?"

"She's playing catch-up," she said. "Everyone else is already in."

"Thought so." I went to the door leading into the main office at the back. As I entered, the printer sang a greeting to the tune of 'O Christmas Tree'. Despite it still being in holiday mode, most of the decorations had been taken down while I'd been gone, including the creepy life-sized snowmen the boss had procured for our office party on Christmas Eve.

"Hey," I said to the others.

Bethan waved at me from the desk beside mine, her

pile of paperwork somehow twice as high as mine despite my absence. Since her magical gift involved being able to work much faster than the average person, I suspected she'd taken on the bulk of my workload while I'd been gone.

Opposite me sat Rob, nephew of the chief of the local werewolves, while at his side sat Lizzie, our office's technological expert and the maker of the coffee machine I desperately needed right now. I went to get myself a mug of one of her trademark mood-boosting coffees to wake me up, hoping that it would also kick my brain into gear.

Sitting down at my desk, I picked up the stack of papers, and the word *market* jumped out at me from the first sheet.

"The town's first goblin market is in need of assistants," I read. "What's a goblin market?"

"The goblin market travels between magical towns, and it's coming here this weekend," said Bethan. "It's been roaming all over the region, so we knew it'd be here soon, and we always need extra staff on security duty to make sure nobody causes any trouble."

Hold on. My dad's note had mentioned a market. Might he have known the goblin market was coming to Fairy Falls?

"And it's staffed by goblins," I read.

Goblins were a relation of the fairies, albeit a distant one, and there weren't many living here in Fairy Falls. Not compared to the elves, anyway. But I knew of no other markets in the area.

"The goblins run the show," said Lizzie. "But the market picks up people as it moves between locations.

Since people come from all over to visit the market, it's always good for local businesses."

"So I have to call these business owners and ask if they want to take part?" I scanned the list in front of me.

"Most of them will already know about the market, so it's a fairly straightforward job," said Bethan. "I thought it'd be easier for you to start off with that, since our other client is that eccentric wizard from Manchester who insists on making all his potential employees memorise a hundred-page rulebook before their interview."

"Yeah, I'd much rather deal with goblins over that guy." I turned to the list and busied myself with the tasks of the day, trying not to dwell on my dad's note any more than I had to. *Start with the market,* he'd said. Assuming he'd meant the goblin market, it shouldn't be hard to pay a visit there once it showed up in Fairy Falls.

And if it was as popular as the others claimed, then nobody would have to know my plan to get hold of a Pixie-Glass and contact my father.

————

After work, I headed to my first magic lesson of the new year. I took classes in the evenings several days a week, alongside Rebecca, the region's current Head Witch. At eleven, she was the all-time youngest witch to ever hold the title, and she'd been chosen by the ceremonial sceptre by complete accident when someone else had stolen it from the hands of the last Head Witch. I'd taken a liking to Rebecca, since she was one of few people who understood my outsider status. She'd grown up under the thumb of her terrifying mother, who'd exploited her magical ability to influence people's personalities merely by looking them in the eye. I'd seen to Mrs Dailey's imprisonment, and as a result, Rebecca and I had bonded. Since nobody else was behind enough in their magical education to join me in my lessons, Rebecca and I took after-school classes together.

I entered the large brick building that housed the leading witch coven and made my way to the usual class-room. Rita, the red-haired witch who ran my classes, waved a bangled arm at me from the front of the room. Rebecca herself already sat in the front row, the Head Witch's ceremonial sceptre propped against her chair.

"How was your holiday, Blair?" asked Rita. "I hope you're ready to get back to lessons."

"Great, thank you," I said. "I'm ready to start."

Not exactly true. I'd taken a break from anything work-related while I'd been away with Nathan, and now my brain felt like a leaky faucet, as far as my magical knowledge was concerned.

To say my magical education had been riddled with bumps was like saying gargoyles were a little grumpy. I was a natural at some kinds of magic—like my innate ability to tell what type of paranormal someone was at first glance, and to sense whether someone was telling the truth or not—but inconsistent with others. Like most everyday branches of magic, for instance. If my emotions ran high, my sense of control flew out the window, so I'd need to put all thoughts of Dad's letter and my foster parents' return to the country from my mind if I wanted to perform well.

"Good, because we have a lot of ground to cover," said Rita. "Starting with your Grade Four training. This is going to be a little different than your magical education so far."

I'd expected as much. Grade Four covered the ages from nine through twelve, while Grade Five went up to sixteen. That meant I'd have more tests and hoops to jump through than I'd encountered previously, without ascending a grade until I'd mastered some pretty advanced spells. Right now, I was struggling to remember how to cast a basic unlocking charm. Why hadn't I thought to recap my last term's studies last night? Oh, right, because I'd been trying to think of ways to entertain my foster parents without letting on that I spent my evenings learning how to turn hats into hares. *Focus, Blair.*

"The Grade Four testing is divided into four sections," she went on. "Like Grade Three, you'll have a practical exam and a theory one, as well as testing in alchemy and potion-making. However, your theory exam will be broken into sections, including new modules on magical history and other subjects. Your practical test will also cover some basic hexes as well as the spells you're accustomed to. You'll be learning more advanced techniques, as well as how to work with a partner. And finally, you'll have to pick one specialist area to focus on."

I should had guessed there'd be a catch. My last 'specialist' test had involved trying to mount a broomstick and humiliating myself in front of a bunch of schoolchildren. I'd barely passed the actual exam, but the alternatives were trying to get Sky to act like a witch's familiar or learning some other skill I'd never tried before. I'd need to think about that one. Rebecca wasn't far behind me, but she'd likely catch up to her peers by the end of the school year, which would bring an end to our magical lessons together. Still, that was months away, and we had a lot of material to cover in the meantime. The sheer size of this year's textbook was proof of that.

"However," said Rita, "I've decided to adapt your curriculum to take into account your current circumstances. That means you, Rebecca."

"You mean being Head Witch?" asked Rebecca. "Why? I thought the tests I passed would be enough."

"They're enough to satisfy the council," she said, "but soon, you'll be touring the local witch communities. I think it would be prudent to cover some groundwork in defensive spells, and Blair, too, would benefit from being able to defend herself with magic. You know how to use spells in self-defence, yes, but you haven't covered any magical shields or wards yet."

Nope, because if they go wrong, they blow up in my face. But I knew where she was coming from. Many coven members resented the fact that Rebecca had been chosen as Head Witch, so knowing how to defend herself would come in handy. As for me, the level of trouble I attracted was higher than almost everyone else in town.

"What do you think, Blair?" she asked.

"Okay," I said. "I'll give it a go."

"Good." Rita raised her wand. "I will demonstrate a basic shielding spell."

Rita waved her wand in a zigzag motion. I watched her, trying to memorise the movement. Then she repeated the spell again. "Rebecca, I'd suggest using your wand at first and switching to the sceptre once you've got the hang of the basics."

"All right." Rebecca pulled out her own wand, and the two of us prepared to follow Rita's lead.

I waved my wand in a zigzag motion, and a jet of glittering light shot out the end of my wand, fizzling out upon contact with the wall.

"That wasn't a shield, Blair," said Rita. "You need to give it more force—without the jabbing motion."

She walked between us, correcting our movements as we practised over and over again. You wouldn't think there'd be much potential for destruction in a spell designed for self-defence, but I managed to knock over the desk three times, even so.

After a few minutes of practise, Rita called us to attention. "Now it's time to pair up. Stand here—out of range of the desks—and try to keep your wands pointed at one another to minimise the risk. You'll have to take it in turns. One of you will aim an offensive spell at the other —try to keep it a mild one, like levitation—and the other will conjure a shield to repel it."

I stepped out in front of Rebecca, gripping my wand in my hand. Since she'd passed the inspection on the solstice and had been assessed by the leaders of the regional witch covens, Rebecca would be starting her meetings with the other local witch communities soon, and I knew she was nervous about representing the whole town. I had to do my best for her.

Rebecca raised her wand and fired a spell at me. I waved mine in defence, but instead of conjuring a shield, a jet of glitter shot from my wand, splattering the wall.

Rita vanished it with a wave of her own wand. "Really, Blair."

"Sorry," I said. "I guess I'm a bit out of practise."

Maybe my wand was rusty from lack of use. I gave it a slight shake, and more glitter trickled out the end. I tried to pretend I'd done it on purpose and faced Rebecca with a smile. "I'm ready."

Rebecca executed a perfect levitation spell. I swooped high into the air and would have cracked my head on the ceiling if I hadn't switched on my levitating boots at the last second. Flipping over in mid-air, I caught my balance and floated back to earth.

"Blair, remember to actually wave your wand next time," Rita said in exasperated tones. "Relax, Blair, and focus on Rebecca."

Once more, Rebecca waved her wand. I moved mine in retaliation, and a rush of air escaped the end of my wand, rattling the shelves.

"Slower, Blair," she reprimanded. "If you move that fast, you'll be lucky to keep hold of your wand."

"Sorry." I hung my head.

She exhaled in a sigh. "Switch positions. Blair, you cast a spell on Rebecca. Rebecca, defend yourself."

I took aim, seeing Rebecca's obvious nerves, and waved my wand. As I did so, a shrieking noise came from outside, and my balance slipped. My spell bounced off the wall, leaving a dent in the plaster. Rebecca, meanwhile, dropped her own wand on the floor.

Rita pursed her lips. With a flick of her wand, she sealed the hole in the wall. It wasn't the first time one of us had hit the wall instead of our intended target.

The shrieking noise struck up again, louder. It sounded like a person, screaming in pain.

"Someone's hurt out there." I made for the door, Rebecca on my heels, and peered out of the classroom just as the front doors to the building burst open.

A man came staggering into the entrance hall,

shrieking at the top of his voice. He had a mop of auburn hair and his eyes were wide with terror. From the look of his clothes, he'd had a swim in the lake and then rolled around in the mud, yet my paranormal-sensing power didn't peg him as a werewolf.

Rita pushed past me into the entrance hall, aiming her wand at the intruder.

"Excuse me!" Rita said. "You're disturbing my classes. What are you doing?"

He jabbed a finger at me. "You're all monsters."

Well. That wasn't what I needed to hear, especially in my human form. "Who are you?"

"They're chasing me!" He spun on the spot, pointing wildly at some invisible enemy. "They're going to kill me."

With a lurching movement, he ran for the stairs. Rita marched to intercept him before he went barging up into Madame Grey's private rooms. "Stop this at once!" she commanded.

He jerked away from her, stumbling backwards onto the carpet and shedding leaves everywhere. "You're monsters!"

"Believe me, we aren't." I walked closer, though I hadn't the faintest idea what I was supposed to do. He wasn't threatening anyone, just yelling at the top of his lungs and clearly terrified out of his mind. Heads poked out of the other classrooms as the noise drew the attention of the other witches and wizards.

The stranger whirled on me and jabbed a finger in my direction. "Wings, wings!"

Instinctively, I twisted my head around to look over my shoulder—but my wings were invisible, as they always were when I was in my human form. "What wings?"

"You're one of them!" he yelled. "They're everywhere."

He could see my wings? That couldn't be right. Nobody was supposed to be able to see through my glamour. No human was, anyway.

Strangely, my paranormal-sensing power still hadn't kicked in. Usually, it went off the instant I laid eyes on someone, so reliable that by now it had become background noise. But for him, there was no response.

"Okay, that's enough." Rita waved her wand, and he keeled over, unconscious. "Clearly, someone put a spell on him. Does anyone know who he is?"

Confused murmurs came from the students peering out of the classrooms. I was sure I'd never seen him before, and while he lay unconscious on the ground, my paranormal-sensing power remained quiet. Even with the Inquisitor, who I hadn't been able to read, I'd picked up on *something,* even if I hadn't been able to tell what he was.

"Who is he?" asked Rebecca. "He's not a wizard."

He wasn't dressed like one, but then again, neither was I. Only those in positions of authority wore anything resembling a uniform. Like Madame Grey, for instance. "I don't know."

"Madame Grey isn't in," said Rita, "but this is not a matter for her to deal with. Unless he's a wizard, which I doubt."

"Then what are you going to do with him?" I asked.

"I'll take him to the hospital," she said. "He seems confused and disorientated, and even if he's under a simple spell, they'll be able to reverse it without disturbing Madame Grey. Rebecca, stay behind, and if you see your grandmother, send her my way. Blair, come with me."

She flicked her wand, levitating the man through the oak doors and out into the street. Despite his dishevelled appearance, he didn't look injured. Yet why hadn't my paranormal-sensing power responded to him?

Alissa was working the evening shift up at the hospital, so I sent her a quick text as we made our way out of the witches' headquarters. Another flick of Rita's wand, and the stranger floated alongside us, up the high street and into the brick building that housed the town's hospital for magical injuries.

We entered the reception area, where Rita flagged down a passing nurse and asked her to fetch Alissa. After a moment, Alissa ran out of a side room.

"Hey, Blair," she said. "What's wrong with that guy?"

"We found him running around the witches' headquarters, raving," Rita explained. "I believe he's under a spell, or under the effects of some hallucinatory substance. Since he was behaving erratically, I thought it would be best to bring him here. For his own safety, as well as others."

"Okay," said Alissa. "I'll see what I can do with him."

When she waved her wand, the man's eyes flew open, and he screamed, "Monsters!"

"What's your name?" Alissa asked the stranger.

In answer, he let out an unintelligible yell.

"Where do you come from?" asked Alissa. "Are you from Fairy Falls? Or Fox Hollow?"

"Monsters!" he screamed. "Nothing but monsters!"

Her brow furrowed. "All right, lie still. I'll make the monsters go away."

He shook his head. "You can't. You can't!"

"Hold on." Alissa moved in, and with a flick of her

wand, he fell unconscious again. "I'll get him somewhere he can't disturb the other patients."

She levitated him through a door and into one of the wards, while I remained behind with Rita. "He's not from Fairy Falls, but where is he from? Do you know?"

"I doubt he's from a local coven," said Rita. "If he was a wizard, he'd have tried to use magic in self-defence by now if he really feared for his safety. I'll fetch Madame Grey, and she'll get to the bottom of this."

"Is my lesson over, then?" I asked.

"Yes, it is," she said. "I doubt this matter will help your concentration, Blair."

No kidding. A stranger raving about monsters wasn't even in the top ten of my weirdest experiences in Fairy Falls, but I could count on one hand the number of times my paranormal-sensing power had failed to respond to someone. On at least one of those occasions, the person in question had been dead, but it even worked on the *un*dead. Vampires, anyway. Not ghosts, though, but this guy was as solid as me. He wasn't a fairy, I was sure, but something about him bothered me in a way I couldn't put my finger on. Something other than his raving about me being a monster, that is.

After a few minutes, the front door opened, and Madame Grey entered the waiting room. Tall and imposing, she wore her white hair braided down her back over her trademark grey cloak and her horn-rimmed spectacles were perched on the end of her nose.

"Blair," she said. "I'm told you found a stranger under the influence of a spell?"

"I don't know who he is," I replied. "Nobody does. All

we know is that he's not from Fairy Falls, or he believes he isn't. He's with Alissa."

She strode ahead into the corridor. I hesitated, then followed her. While I wasn't really allowed into the patients' rooms without permission, the stranger had seen my wings, and I wanted to find out why.

"I can't read him," I told Madame Grey. "I mean, my paranormal-sensing power isn't working on him."

"Is that so?" She arched a brow. "I'll see what my granddaughter says."

The man's yells made it easy to find his room. He huddled in the corner, while Alissa and two other nurses stood over him, wands in their hands.

"Madame Grey." Alissa backed up to her grandmother's side, dropping her voice. "No spell will work on him while he's unconscious, but he's completely insensible. He won't tell us who he is or where he came from. I'm not sure he actually knows, to be honest."

Madame Grey studied him. "You say your paranormal-sensing ability isn't working, Blair?"

"It isn't?" asked Alissa.

I shook my head. "Sometimes it can't figure someone out, but rarely." I didn't want to bring up the fairies yet, not with an audience. "I don't know what the problem is."

"There's a simple way to get to the bottom of this." Madame Grey conjured up a small flame in mid-air. Then she conjured a slip of paper and cast it into the flame. The fire devoured the paper until nothing remained but the smell of burning cloves.

"He's not one of us," said Madame Grey.

She didn't mean he wasn't a wizard. The man was a normal. Not a paranormal at all.

Impossible.

The man screamed, "Monsters!"

"Can you calm him down?" Alissa said to Lou, one of her fellow nurses. "I need to talk to my grandmother."

I followed her and Madame Grey out into the corridor. While part of me was relieved that the lack of reaction from my paranormal-sensing power had a simple explanation, his presence here in Fairy Falls unnerved me. It wasn't supposed to be possible for anyone to just wander in—though admittedly, I'd done exactly that myself the first time I'd come here. If someone had spelled him *and* brought him to town, though, they'd broken at least a dozen of the paranormal world's most stringent rules.

"How'd he get here?" I whispered to Alissa.

"I don't know, but he's definitely under some kind of enchantment." Alissa closed the door behind her. "He didn't respond to any of our reversal charms, either. It's more complex than it looks."

"Especially if he found his way here without help," said Madame Grey. "He saw through the town's enchantments. Most normals who try to get close end up passing over the town altogether."

Of course. It'd slipped my mind, given how quickly I'd adjusted to living here, but the first time I'd stepped into Fairy Falls had been accidental because I literally couldn't see the place until I was already behind its wards. Powerful enchantments drove away any intruders who didn't have magical origins.

"Are you positive he isn't at least partially paranormal?" I asked Madame Grey. "Because he also saw my fairy wings."

Which made no sense. Normal humans couldn't see through glamour. Even witches and other paranormals couldn't. It wasn't supposed to be possible.

"He did?" Her eyes rounded behind her glasses. "No… the tests are never wrong. Even in your case, Blair, we found answers. But that's very troubling."

"He saw your wings?" said Alissa. "How?"

"Don't ask me." Something was definitely up. He couldn't have found his way here alone. Not without help. "Has a normal ever wandered into Fairy Falls before? I mean, except for me."

Fairy Falls didn't even appear on maps, and when I'd been on my way here for the first time, the bus I'd taken had broken down miles away, leaving me to trek through the fields until I'd found some signs of civilisation.

"It's rare," said Madame Grey. "Very rare. When it occurs, it's generally because someone unintentionally left a gap in our security or invited a friend here. If he has friends in Fairy Falls, though, it looks like they abandoned him."

"Should I ask Nathan to send someone to check the border?" I asked.

"That would be a wise idea, Blair," she said. "In the meantime, we can't have him spreading our secrets to other normals. We'll have to come up with a workable plan to remove him from town and place him back in the world he belongs in—once he's recovered from the spell afflicting him, that is."

"Can't you erase his memory?" I asked. "With a… what do you call it, a Mind-Wiper?"

"They're only available from the highest authorities," she said. "Meaning, the regional coven leaders. We only just passed their examination, and the last thing we want is for them to find someone from our community may have violated the law and invited an ordinary human into our world."

"Not to mention we don't know what spell he's under," added Alissa. "Without removing it, it's too dangerous to send him back into the normal world unsupervised. He might end up spreading the effect to others or causing them to find their way here to Fairy Falls, too."

My heart lurched. It wasn't his fault he was here, and if the regional witch council found out, it was Madame Grey who'd take the heat for it. Not to mention the town's council… and poor Rebecca, already carrying the weight of the world on her eleven-year-old shoulders.

But if someone was revealing the magical world to outsiders, the entire town might face the consequences.

3

On my way home, I texted Nathan asking him if he could send out a team to the border to look around for more runaway humans before our date tonight. Half of me expected Steve to send Nathan out himself and force him to cancel our date—again—but luck was with me for once and he responded saying he wasn't due to go out until later.

I met Nathan at our favourite pub, the Troll's Tavern, where we ordered our food and drinks by tapping the menu and it appeared on the table a few minutes later. Some things in the magical world were complicated, but I really appreciated the small conveniences.

"I'm glad Steve didn't send you out there," I said, hearing the pattering of rain on the windows outside. "It sucks that you have to go out later, though."

"I think I got off easy, considering," said Nathan. "I've spent the last day catching up on paperwork, so I wouldn't mind getting outside for a bit. If I didn't know better, I'd say Steve saved every piece of paperwork in the whole office for my return."

"Wouldn't surprise me." I dug into my meal. "Didn't he take the whole of last week off to spend time with his mistress?"

The idea of someone wanting to date the grumpy gargoyle boggled the mind, but it seemed life was as illogical in the magical world as it was in the normal one. The gargoyle police chief had never quite forgiven Nathan for taking over his security team—even though it'd been Steve who'd hired him as a security guard in the first place—and took every opportunity to make trouble for him. He wasn't much of a fan of me, either.

"You've got it," he said. "In fact, Clare told me he showed up back to work a day late and someone had to cover for him. Luckily, I missed that debacle."

"All this talk of Steve's girlfriend is ruining my appetite." I jabbed a fork into my baked potato. "Anyway, as you probably gathered from my text, the curse of Blair has started already. A normal wandered into town, and nobody knows how he got here or where he came from."

A frown puckered his brow. "I heard a stranger showed up at the witches' headquarters. I should have guessed you were involved."

"It's a law of the magical world." I took a sip of my drink. "Whenever anything weird shows up, it gravitates towards me. I suppose I should be grateful everyone else had a nice break while we were gone."

Nathan shot me a smile. "Hey, we managed a fairly stress-free holiday."

"You're conveniently forgetting the fact that someone died at the hotel we stayed at." Even on holiday, trouble dogged my steps. But a human wandering into town was a new one. The laws against exposing the paranormal world were strict enough that it'd taken me twenty-five years to even guess *I* was magical.

He sipped his beer. "I said 'fairly' stress-free for a reason."

"Or 'fairy'," I added. "Speaking of which, our visitor freaked out when he saw me and called me a monster, which really wasn't what I wanted to hear today. Also, I think he saw my wings."

His brow furrowed. "He saw your wings? Isn't that…"

"Impossible," I finished. "Even Madame Grey can't figure out how he did it."

"She's looking into it?" he said. "If she's involved, I've no doubt she'll get to the bottom of it."

"I don't know of any spell that can cause someone to suddenly develop the ability to see through fairy glamour, though." I chewed a mouthful meditatively. "I'll ask Alissa when I'm home. She and the other staff at the hospital are having to deal with our visitor, but they can't risk letting him out in case he wanders back home and tells everyone about the paranormal world."

This was not a good time for me to be considering introducing my own foster parents to the magical world, that was for sure. Imagining their reactions to my fairy wings was worse than imagining Steve with a girlfriend, if possible.

"I expect once they figure out what spell is on him, it should be easy to reintroduce him to the normal world," he said. "It's not the first case I've heard of, though it hasn't happened since I moved to Fairy Falls."

"Forgetting someone?" I gave a smile, though my mind

was half on my foster parents. "Speaking of which, I need to make plans to see my foster parents without exposing them to this madness. They're back in the country and they want to meet you, so I'm afraid you're my cover story as to why I've been gone the last few months."

"That's fine," he said. "It's true, isn't it? I was the first person you met here."

"Yeah." A smile tugged at my mouth at the memory. "You kinda scared me at first, I won't lie."

Dressed in hunter gear, Nathan had found me wandering around near the lake, unwittingly trespassing in a town I wasn't supposed to be able to see. Ever since that day, I'd wondered if anyone else had ever arrived in the magical world the same way, but the new stranger's situation was a different matter entirely.

He smiled back. "I hope I've made a better impression since then."

"Don't worry, you have," I said lightly. "So… want to meet my foster parents?"

"I'm free this weekend if you are," said Nathan. "Whereabouts were you thinking of meeting them?"

"Sloan, which is about an hour's walk from Fairy Falls," I said. "I'm still trying to figure out a cover story as to why they can't come here, but we can meet up with them at a coffee shop or something. Pretty sure that's far enough from the magical world to avoid trouble. Unless a pixie shows up again."

"I can't imagine a pixie would want to hang around a normal town," he said. "Technology and magic don't mix."

"Yeah, I always wondered why I didn't get on with public transport," I said. "It felt like every bus I got on broke down within half an hour, and once I made an entire office of computers crash at the same time. I just figured I was cursed with bad luck."

Bad luck aside, there were a dozen reasons I faced my foster parents' visit with trepidation. After all, I wasn't the same person I'd been the last time we'd seen one another. I lived a literal world away, and as for everything I'd found out about my birth parents? I couldn't mention any of that to them. It was too risky.

"You needed to find the place you really belonged in," he said. "Your parents will see you're happy here without needing to know all the details."

"It feels like tempting fate," I admitted. "Bringing them into my world right after another normal ended up in trouble."

"I'm sure that was a one-off," he said. "It's very rare for normals to experience anything related to the magical world."

No kidding. I'd managed twenty-five years without it, but I'd had no known links with the paranormal world beforehand. My foster parents *did* have a link… me. And I attracted more magical trouble than the average person on a good day. My technology-destroying ways might have ebbed, but my bad-luck-magnet nature remained somewhere between unfortunate and the backlash of a Lucky Latte.

Still. As far as families went, I'd struck gold with Mr and Mrs Wilkes, and the very least I could do was give them an insight into my new life, even an incomplete one. Better that than cutting them out of my life entirely.

Nathan walked me home after our meal, kissing me goodnight on the doorstep.

"I'd better hurry to the police station before Steve starts nagging me," he said.

I pulled a face. "Making you patrol in the cold doesn't seem fair. It's not like you have wings and leathery gargoyle skin to keep you warm out there."

"I'll be fine." He drew me into an embrace and brushed a strand of hair from my forehead. "See you tomorrow?"

"Sure." I released him, my heart giving a happy leap. My life might be as chaotic as ever, but Nathan kept me on an even keel.

I went inside the flat to find Alissa had returned from her shift at the hospital. She sat on the sofa with a cat curled up on either side of her.

"Hey." She waved sleepily at me. "Good date?"

"Sure." I went to join her. "It'd be better if Steve wasn't working Nathan off his feet to get him back for disappearing for a week, but he's free to come and meet my foster parents this weekend."

I'd call them tomorrow and make a plan. For now… it was time for me to tell Alissa something else I'd been sitting on for weeks.

"Where are you going to meet?" she asked.

"Sloan, the town between Fairy Falls and where they live." I squeezed onto the sofa next to my cat and gave Sky a stroke. "I'm still working on my cover story, but I'm pretending I moved to Sloan and not here. It's all very well for me to visit them or meet somewhere for the day, but sooner or later they'll want to know where I'm living, and I can't very well tell them it's a place that isn't visible on any ordinary map."

"There are spells…" She hesitated. "But I won't force you to use them. It's a personal choice."

"You mean spells that will erase their memories of our meeting?" I guessed.

"Nothing that drastic," she said. "I mean spells that will stop them from asking the wrong questions."

I shook my head. "I don't want to manipulate them in any way. But that means I'll have to work on an airtight cover story."

"The town's magic helps," she said. "If anyone tries to walk here, they end up getting turned around and forgetting where they are, in a way that feels totally natural."

"Except for that guy we met today, apparently."

She grimaced. "We can't figure out what spell was used on him. If we could do that, we might have an idea of who brought him here. Until then, we can't risk letting him go."

"I guess not." I stroked Sky again, wondering how to broach the subject of the fairies. Part of the problem was that it involved secrets that weren't mine, and which might spell consequences for more than just myself.

My phone buzzed with a message from Erin, Nathan's sister. *Back in town. Wanna go to the market tomorrow?*

"Tomorrow?" I echoed. "I thought the market wasn't coming to town until the weekend."

"Who's messaging you?" asked Alissa. "The market's in Fox Hollow, the next town over."

"Buck must still be staying there," I concluded. "Erin wants to go and check out the market tomorrow."

"Any reason?" she said. "She just wants to hang out?"

"Guess she's back in town." The last time we'd all been in the same place, it'd ended with Nathan, Erin and Buck all being suspects in a murder case. While they'd all been cleared, I'd faced Erin's return from visiting her family over the holidays with trepidation. On the other hand, it gave me an excuse to go to the market early and ask about the Pixie-Glass without risking running into people I knew.

"Blair?" Alissa waved a hand in front of my face. "You're spacing out. What's up?"

"My dad's note…" I paused. "It said *you might want to start with the market.* Now it turns out the goblin market is coming to town. What are the odds?"

Her mouth formed an *O* of understanding. "You think this Pixie-Glass might be at the market? They do have a lot of weird magical stuff you can't buy anywhere else, so it's worth checking out. Is that why Erin wants to go?"

"I didn't tell her about my dad's note, so I don't know." Buck had been staying in Fox Hollow while he and Erin looked for work in or near Fairy Falls, so he must still be there. Sky crawled into my lap to demand a stroke and I used the interruption as a chance to draw my thoughts together.

"What is it, Blair?" Alissa leaned forward in her seat. "I know you need to find the Pixie-Glass so you can talk to your dad, but well… do you really want to get involved with the hunters again? Not counting Nathan, I mean. I know Erin quit, but her fiancé…"

"I don't know if Buck is still an active hunter or not." I drew in a breath. "But he's a fairy. Like me."

A heartbeat passed. "Seriously?"

"Yes, and I don't know if I'm allowed to tell anyone or not," I admitted. "Erin didn't act like it's a big deal, but only she and Nathan knew, the last I heard. If he moves to Fairy Falls, though, people will figure it out. Oh, and Blythe knows, too. She's the one who pointed it out."

"*Blythe?*" she said. "How would she know?"

"I'm not a hundred percent certain," I said, "but I think her mother told her."

"Mrs Dailey worked with the hunters." She gave a nod of understanding, her expression concerned. "Buck isn't working with her, is he?"

"I doubt it, considering she's in jail, and good riddance." My hands clenched, and I accidentally grabbed a handful of Sky's fur in the process, prompting an angry hiss. "But there's a reason my paranormal-sensing powers bounced clean off him. I can't identify other fairies. Not if they don't want me to."

Silence spread between us as the implication sank in.

"The *Inquisitor*," she breathed.

"I don't know if he's told anyone or not." I stroked Sky, the repetitive motion soothing my nerves a little. "I don't know how to deal with it, either. Nathan was shocked when I told him, and I'd be surprised if his dad knows. The other hunters—I assume some of them must know, but it's all guesswork. I can't imagine it's a widely known fact that the guy in charge of the paranormal hunters is a fairy, but I'm at a loss as to what it all means."

"Your dad." Her eyes widened. "Is it linked to why he was arrested?"

"Maybe." I looked down. "I didn't realise how risky it was for him to send pixies to deliver messages, but it explains why he stopped. The Inquisitor can see through other fairies' glamour."

"So that's why your dad wants you to find the Pixie-Glass instead," she said. "And Buck… do you reckon he and Erin will help you? At the market?"

"I hope so." I looked back at her. "But—the guy in the

hospital saw through my glamour, too. Is there a spell that can do that?"

"No." Her mouth pinched with concern. "There isn't, not a witch spell anyway."

Then only one explanation was left... the stranger who'd come to town was under a fairy spell.

My focus at work the next day was scattered, to say the least. Erin and I had arranged to meet at the market after my shift finished, but I still had yet to call my foster parents and make definite plans for the weekend. On top of the human stranger's arrival and my mission to find a way to contact my dad, it was a wonder I had any attention span left to deal with clients at all.

As I left work, a message came through from Alissa telling me to meet her at the hospital. *Did something else happen?*

I hurried up along the high street to the hospital and found Alissa hovering inside the waiting room. "Hey, Blair," she said. "Are you still going to the market?"

"That was the plan," I said. "Why?"

"We have a situation." She turned aside as a door opened and an elf sidled into the waiting room. His arm was bound in a sling and a bandage was wrapped around his head, covering one pointed ear. "You're not supposed to be wandering around, Thistle. Get back to your bed."

I recognised the patient as a notorious local elf with a drinking problem who was forever getting himself into scrapes. The elf looked blearily at Alissa and me. "Oh, it's you."

"He's drunk," Alissa said in an undertone. "Idiot managed to fall off a cliff and break a few bones. Not the first time, but he's yet to sober up and it's been more than a day."

"Blame the goblins," he said. "Goblins, nasty creatures, they are."

"Fine, then," she said. "You can talk to Blair in here."

The sound of screaming rose from behind a nearby door. "Monsters, monsters!"

I looked between Alissa and the elf, nonplussed. "What did you want him to talk to me about? Our new guest?"

"Kind of." Her expression darkened, and she beckoned the elf into view. "This absolute genius went on a bender last night and got so wasted that he ended up lost in Sloan. He was found wandering around the street in front of a bunch of normals, pointed ears and all."

"How dare you insult me!" he said, addressing a potted plant instead of Alissa.

Alissa rolled her eyes. "Anyway, it sounds like our new arrival is from the same area. I wondered if you could ask Thistle here a couple of questions, Blair, if it's not too much trouble. I have no idea if anything he says is the truth."

"Oh, sure." I checked the time. I had a few minutes to spare before I had to meet Erin and Buck. "Thistle... that's your name, right?"

"Who, I?" He fell over, grabbing the plant for balance. "Nasty goblins did this, they did. Not I."

"Did what?" I asked. "Got you drunk?"

Goblin market. Hang on...

"Yes, I partook of their dreadful brew, and into dreams

I dove." He nearly did dive into the potted plant, but he caught himself at the last second.

"Were you at the market?" I asked. "Is that where you got into trouble?"

"Trouble?" said the elf. "Never."

"You were found wandering around a normal town in front of non-magical folk, singing at the top of your lungs," said Alissa. "You didn't put a spell on a normal while you were at it, did you?"

"No!" he said. "Not at all."

True. When Alissa caught my eye, I shook my head a little, and Alissa pursed her lips. "You didn't answer Blair's question. Were you at the market?"

He hiccoughed. "The goblins don't like the elves, not at all, but I tipped handsomely. Now, I see rainbows."

"Does that drink cause hallucinations?" I asked suspiciously. "What did you drink?"

"Goblin brew, of course of course." He sat down on the floor, leaning against the wall. "I see what nobody else ever saw. Goblin brew bestows upon you the true sight, do you know what I mean?"

"True sight?" I echoed, a sudden suspicion dawning on me. "Can goblin brew make anyone gain the ability to see through glamour? Even—even a normal?"

The elf grinned. "I'll tell you if you bring me a cocktail from the Laughing Pixie."

"Nice try," Alissa said. "There's a human next door in an intoxicated state—a *normal.* Did you give him goblin brew?"

"I do not share my drinks, never," he said solemnly. "I remember nothing more. Let me see my pretty rainbow lights in peace."

"Then go back to your ward." Alissa beckoned to him, a stern undercurrent to her voice. "If you let me use a healing spell on you, I might discharge you early, but if I find out you committed any crimes while you were running amok through Sloan, you'll find yourself up for a stint behind bars."

He rose to his feet shakily, tottering around. "Yes, cruel human, I will oblige."

It took him several attempts to get through the door to the ward, and a crash and a yelp followed as he tripped over the threshold and fell flat on his face.

Alissa muttered a curse under her breath. "Personally, I think a night in a cell would stop his habit of causing havoc, but I'll settle for locking him in the ward instead. Thanks for questioning him, Blair."

"No problem," I said. "So… goblin brew. Should I look for that at the market?"

"If you can. I'm stuck here all night." She grimaced. "I'm sure you'll be fine, Blair. You aren't a normal, and you aren't prone to getting into trouble either. I mean, not as much as certain people."

"I heard that!" bellowed the elf from the other side of the door.

"Looks like you have your hands full," I said. "Want me to come back to question him again while he's sober? Just on the off-chance that he does know how our new guest ended up in that state?"

"That'd be great," she said. "I'll have to wait for him to sober up to confirm if he does know anything about our poor lost human. We're calling him Riff, because we don't know his name."

I checked the time. "I need to meet Erin, but I'll see you later."

"If you can find out what this goblin brew is, you'll save me a lot of hassle," she said. "I know goblins have a reputation for causing trickery, but selling drinks to humans is forbidden even in their markets."

"I'll see if I can find out if anyone saw the human at the market, too," I said.

"Thanks," she said. "I wish I could come with you, but I have to help old Ava with her pills. Wish me luck."

"Good luck." I waved goodbye and left the hospital to meet Erin.

Goblin brew. Might the human have wandered into the market by accident and been handed a beverage by someone who didn't know any better? It was as good a guess as any, but if someone had lured him to the market on purpose, they could be arrested for it. Thistle claimed to be innocent, but the fact that he'd ran around drunk in front of a group of humans was downright alarming. It was lucky he hadn't happened to be staggering around the streets of Sloan on the same day my foster parents and I planned to meet.

Whatever the case, if normals were being drawn into this world, it might affect my foster parents next. For their sakes, I had to figure out the truth.

4

———

Nathan's sister Erin waited for me outside the local coffee shop, Charms & Caffeine. She wore muddy boots and jeans with ragged edges, as though she'd trekked here through the muddiest route possible. At her side stood Buck, who wore similar attire. Nothing about his blue eyes, pale gold hair and fine-boned features hinted at his fairy nature. Like me, he wore a glamour that made him look entirely human.

"Hey," I said. "Nice to see you back in town, Erin. And you, Buck."

"Hey, Blair," said Buck. "Ready to head to the market?"

"You bet." I fell into step alongside Erin, while Buck took the lead uphill through the town's centre. "Is the market going to stay in Fox Hollow before it moves to Fairy Falls this weekend?"

"Technically, it's in a field in the middle of nowhere," said Erin. "Did you say there's something you want to look for at the market?"

"Yeah." I was starting to wish I'd figured out a cover

story. I'd been desperate to speak to Buck for ages about the hunters' relationship with the fairies, but for all I knew, he and Erin hadn't the faintest idea of the Inquisitor's real nature. Erin and Buck weren't that high up among the hunters, even before they'd left, but that didn't mean the Inquisitor wouldn't find out if I'd been asking questions about him. I couldn't be a hundred percent sure Buck hadn't cut ties with the hunters—and Erin definitely hadn't, given how deep her family was involved with them.

"What did you want to look for?" asked Buck.

"There's a guy we found wandering around town who's under the influence of something he might have obtained from the market," I said, deciding to save my questions on the Inquisitor and the paranormal hunters until later. "He's a normal, without any ties to the magical world, so Madame Grey wants to keep it quiet."

"Someone at the market's targeting normals?" Erin's eyes widened. "First I've heard, but I can ask around."

"Same." Buck glanced at me, his expression unreadable. He couldn't sense I wasn't being entirely truthful, could he? He didn't have lie-sensing powers. My abilities came about due to the unique combination of my mum's witch magic and my dad's fairy magic. Buck was either all fairy or part ordinary human, from what I'd figured.

"A local elf mentioned something called goblin brew," I added. "Does that ring a bell?"

"Sure, I've heard of it," said Buck. "Strong stuff, that. You say an elf mentioned it?"

"Yeah, a local," I said. "He hinted that the human we found might have picked up some of the goblin brew from the market. He saw through my glamour, which can't be the result of a regular spell. I'm inclined to think there's some truth there."

Thistle wasn't exactly the reliable sort, though. Maybe he was lying to cover up the fact that *he'd* given the poor guy the goblin brew. Still, it was worth asking around.

At the word 'glamour', Buck's jaw locked. "That's impossible."

"I thought so," I said. "But it's true. Can this goblin brew stuff really have that effect on normals?"

"I wouldn't know," said Buck. "If an elf told you, he might be lying in order to get the goblins into trouble. They have this weird rivalry, elves and goblins do."

"Really?" Now was my chance. "What about fairies, then? I mean, are they likely to be at the market, too?"

"I don't know," he said. "I've never been before."

"You haven't?" I scrambled for the right words. "Not that there's anything wrong with it. I haven't either. But I assumed, since you're like me..."

"I never met my dad, and he was my fairy parent," he said. "My mum was a normal. I didn't learn anything about them from her."

Wait. He's never met the other fairies? "Then how did you end up working for the hunters?"

"They recruited me from home," he said. "They sent me an invitation to a job interview in the mail when I turned sixteen. I was already looking for a job, so I accepted."

"So is that how you found the paranormal world?" I hadn't known it was possible to be recruited to the hunters if you weren't related to one. Nathan's whole family ran the local branch, so it was a given that he and his siblings would end up being involved in some capacity. But since when did the hunters send out personalised letters to people—specifically, fairies—to recruit them?

"Yeah, turns out my dad put a glamour on me before he took off, so I always assumed I was human," he said. "The truth came out when I got to the interview with the hunters. They gave me a crash course in the paranormal world."

"Wow." I didn't know what else to say. I had an inkling that an introduction to magic from the hunters would be very different than my own magical education from the witches. Then again, what would they have done if I'd been half fairy and half regular human, and not a witch at all?

Erin pointed ahead of us. "Hey, we're here."

We'd reached the goblin market. Brightly coloured tents and stalls filled the whole field, most of them staffed by goblins. Short and green-skinned with pointed ears, they were more rugged and less delicate-looking than elves, though they were of a similar height. Each stall sold a completely different array of goods, from strange spiky fruits to vivid-coloured beverages, glittering jewels and all manner of oddities.

I looked around, taking it all in. On a stretch of hillside set apart from the main market, groups of paranormals danced in circles around a tree, while strange music drifted through the air. I spotted the source—a band consisting of several dazed-looking humans playing various instruments, flutes and fiddles and others I didn't know the name of.

So this was the fairy world in all its dizzying and magical glory. But where in the madness was it possible to find what I was looking for?

Erin nudged me, drawing my attention to a stall with a roof shaped like a crown. Below, a sign said *Goblin Brew,* and a large number of mugs made out of what looked like tree bark covered the table.

I drew in a deep breath. "I hope they aren't as easily offended as the elves are."

I approached the stall, which was staffed by two green-skinned goblins. One peered up at me with pupil-less dark eyes, while the second goblin poured a thick greenish yellow liquid into a mug and offered it to me. "Want some of our special brew?"

"Um." I didn't take the mug. The contents looked about as appetising as drinking raw sewage. "If you don't mind, can you tell me what's in that goblin brew?"

"Why's that?" said his companion.

My mind went blank. The liquid might look foul, but it had a sweet scent that gathered in the back of my throat and made it hard to focus. "I'd rather know if there are going to be any side effects for humans before I drink it."

"Humans?" He let out a raucous laugh. "They're delicate enough that a mere sip will turn them into those poor fools over there."

I followed his gaze to the gathering of dancing figures on the grass in front of the band.

"Are they human?" My heartbeat sped up. What if there were normals among the crowd, like Riff? Maybe I should have brought Nathan with me, but even he didn't have the authority to wield the arm of the magical law outside of Fairy Falls. In fact, I wasn't sure *who* held authority here. "I mean, normals. Not witches. They aren't, are they?"

"It's illegal to sell magical products to normals," said Buck from behind me.

"Normals can't see us," growled the goblin on the left. "Shame, shame… but we're not to sell to normals, they say, so we obey."

As far as my truth-sensing ability was concerned, he was telling the truth, but if they couldn't know for sure if a human was normal or otherwise, perhaps it might have happened by accident. "*Have* you seen any normals here at the market? How many humans normally come here?"

"Lots of humans here," said the right-hand goblin. "And lots of folk who are other than human, too. You're not one of the Court folk, are you?"

"No," I said, confused. "What do you mean by that?"

"Fairies, of course," said the goblin on the left.

"I am," I said. "Half fairy, anyway. But that's not what I'm here to talk to you about. A normal human wandered into our town under the effects of some kind of intoxicating beverage. We think he might have been to the market, so we'd appreciate if you let us know if you saw a human acting strangely."

Both goblins broke into hysterical laughter.

"Strangely?" one of them howled. "This must be your first time at the market."

My face flamed. "Can you just tell me how long the effects of goblin brew last, then?"

"No need for that tone," said the goblin. "For your information, if this human did partake of our beverages, then the effects would be long gone within twenty-four hours."

Huh. It'd been more than a day since the guy in the hospital had shown up in town. Had it not been goblin brew that had caused his hallucinations after all? How, then, had he seen my wings?

"So you definitely didn't sell any of your brew to a human yesterday?" I pressed on. "An elf told me—"

"Oh, so the elves are spreading malicious lies about us again," said the goblin. "They sent someone to snoop around earlier and act as though we're trespassing on their territory just by being here. Woodland elves are so dull."

"They did?" I said. "The elf also said a human who drinks your brew can gain the ability to see through fairy glamour. Is that true?"

"The elves and fairies call it true sight," said the first goblin. "Perhaps humans should see the truth more often." He poured another mug of bright yellow liquid and offered it to Erin.

"No thanks," she said. "What are you saying, then? It can't be anything other than goblin brew that caused a normal to end up with the sight?"

"I did not sell any of my brew to a normal." He turned to me. "Kindly cease with the questions, fairy-human."

True. But my lie-sensing power came with one limit: if someone believed the words they spoke to be true, my ability wouldn't react in the same way as it would if they told a known falsehood. If he hadn't known he was selling to a normal, or someone else had bought the brew and given it to our visitor, my ability wouldn't react.

"Did you see a man dressed in ragged clothes yesterday, then?" I asked.

The second goblin leaned over the table, looking me up and down. "I do not recall it. Now, if you're not going to buy anything, would you kindly move out of the way?"

Resigned, I walked away from the stall and texted Alissa with an update. If I took the goblins at their word, perhaps someone else had been responsible for handing the man the goblin brew. Someone like an intoxicated, mischievous elf, for instance. But then, why had the effects not worn off by now?

"I don't trust them," Buck caught up to me, speaking in a murmur. "The goblins, I mean. Nor the elves, either, come to that. They all get a kick out of pranking humans."

He indicated the dancing, swirling crowd in front of the band. In the midst of the elves and goblins, groups of dazed-looking humans danced wildly, not seeming to notice when their drinks spilt out of their hands.

"I'm not sure we have any authority here," I whispered back. "Does anyone? Like the police in Fox Hollow? Can they intervene if it turns out someone here in the market was responsible for bewitching a human?"

"Technically, the market falls outside local authorities," he said. "Anyone who works here has to abide by the rules of the region as well as the town who is hosting them, but they're smart enough to set it up outside of the actual town so they have more leeway. I could threaten to bring in my supervisor, but I can't exactly follow through on that threat when we're not on speaking terms with one another."

"So you did leave the hunters, then?" I asked.

"I'm on their reserve team." He glanced at Erin. "Until we both find employment in Fairy Falls, anyway. But as I said, my boss and I aren't on speaking terms since I told him I was leaving. Besides, there's not much the hunters can do to stop minor misdemeanours without taking overly harsh measures."

"Like shutting the whole place down," said Erin. "Which is a really great way to end up cursed fifty times over."

My phone buzzed with a reply from Alissa, and I glanced down at her message. "Well, unless our normal managed to smuggle some of the goblin brew into the hospital, it can't be the reason he's still addled. It's not supposed to last more than twenty-four hours, and it's been more than a day since he first showed up in town."

"Maybe he's hiding more under his bed." Erin peered over at the nearest stall, which sold glistening gemstone jewellery. "Hey, I like that necklace, Buck. Hint, hint."

Buck walked behind her to take a closer look, while I texted Alissa again, telling her to search the hospital for any more hidden bottles of goblin brew.

A light caught my eye, shimmering with a glittering purple sheen from somewhere to the left of the jewellery stall. My gaze snagged on a smaller tent selling handmade costumes, and the source of the glittering light: an elegant dress decorated with sequins.

That glow looked familiar to me. Really familiar.

I inched closer, and then halted, disbelieving. Behind the stall stood two people, taller than average with glowing skin and pointed ears and wings. Like my un-glamoured form.

Fairies. They're fairies.

My heartbeat quickened, and for a moment, I remained rooted to the spot, unable to believe they were really here. Fairies. Like me.

Calm down, Blair. You wanted this.

Might they know how to get my hands on a Pixie-

Glass? It was worth asking. I might as well get something useful out of this trip.

I approached the two fairies, who looked at me with curiosity in their gazes. One had long curly blond hair, while the other was a brunette, though their pointed features were identical enough that they might have been siblings.

"Hey," I said. "I wondered—does anyone here know where I might find a Pixie-Glass?"

"How rich do you think we are?" The blond one laughed.

"Oh, it's one of those human-raised fairies." Her companion giggled. "Trust me, you're better off turning back and leaving now, while you can."

"Not happening," I said firmly. "I need a Pixie-Glass to contact someone. It's urgent."

I startled when someone caught my arm and leaned in to speak to me. "I can help you."

I twisted around to look at the newcomer, a male fairy with fair hair and the same pointed features as the two women. He gave me an encouraging smile, beckoning me away from the two giggling fairies.

"Pixie-Glasses are incredibly rare," he murmured. "If you really want to buy one, you'd need a small fortune."

My mouth parted. I might have savings for the first time in my life since I'd moved to Fairy Falls, but I wasn't rich, not by a long shot. Still, Dad wouldn't have set me an impossible task, right?

"Do you know of anyone who has a Pixie-Glass I might be able to borrow, then?" I asked. "I live in Fairy Falls, if it helps."

"You're from *Fairy Falls?*" His eyes rounded. "Well…

there was one incident, some years ago now, when a very rich woman came to purchase a Pixie-Glass from the market. She claimed to be from Fairy Falls."

My throat went dry. *Was it my mother?* "How long ago are we talking about? Can you describe her?"

"Tall brunette," he said. "Not a fairy. A witch, I'd say. Quite unpleasant. What was her name… Mrs Davey?"

Mrs Dailey.

Blythe's mother.

My skin chilled. Mrs Dailey was in jail, but she'd moved away from Fairy Falls long before then. If she'd got her hands on a Pixie-Glass, it'd be just my luck if the hunters had seized it from her when they'd hauled her away. And if *they* had it, I could say goodbye to any chance I might have of contacting my dad.

"Blair!" Buck called from behind me. "C'mon. We have to go."

"Why…" I spun around to see Erin was edging towards the dancers, and by the way Buck was holding onto her with his other hand, his grip alone was preventing her from running off to join them.

I hurried up to help him restrain her. "She didn't drink anything, did she?"

"No," he whispered back, "but I think the music is affecting her."

The eerie melody from the band had grown in volume without my noticing, and now I paid closer attention, the lilting sound became more and more potent. An urge gripped me, to join the others on the dance floor and let all my troubles melt away.

Erin veered in front of me, fighting against Buck's grip. "Let me go. C'mon, Blair, let's dance."

I gave a fierce head-shake to remove the music's influence. "Not a good idea, Erin."

"It's more potent for humans, but fairies tend to be immune." Buck caught Erin's arm again. "Mostly, anyway."

Not quite. The urge continued, but I resisted. Together, we hauled Erin downhill and back towards Fairy Falls. It wasn't until the music faded from hearing distance that Erin finally stopped fighting our grip, and the dazed look in her eyes disappeared.

Erin broke away from Buck. "What happened?"

"Fairy music," said Buck. "Sorry. I didn't know it would have that strong an effect on you."

No wonder the market's folk are the main suspects for what happened to that guy in the hospital. Remembering the two fairies' laughter made a cold pit open inside me. I might be ignorant of my fairy side, but it wasn't through lack of trying, and their dismissal left me feeling wrong-footed. At least the other guy had been helpful, even if he'd given me bad news about my chances of finding a Pixie-Glass.

"Do fairies have an issue with people like us?" I asked Buck. "Fairies who were raised by humans, I mean?"

"They don't acknowledge us as the same as they are," he said, with a grimace of distaste. "I know I *am* one, but the fairies who come here from their own realm play by totally different rules to the rest of us. To be accepted by them, you'd have to leave the human world behind entirely."

"Seriously?" His words struck a sharp chord within me. "That's what they want? And you chose not to?"

"The hunters recruited me before I could face the

choice." He shrugged. "I think I'm better for it, personally. The market isn't really my scene."

"And—" I hesitated. "Have you met many other fairies, since joining the hunters?"

Erin cast a curious look in my direction, but she didn't speak.

"A few," he said. "Why?"

"I just—" I broke off. It seemed to me that Buck didn't know the Inquisitor was a fairy at all, and, moreover, he didn't find it suspicious in the slightest that he'd been personally recruited to the force. After all, why would he? The hunters had shaped his view of the magical world. "I just thought it odd that they'd recruit you before you knew of your fairy nature. I've never heard of it happening to witches."

"Most witches join a coven," he said.

Yeah... but the Inquisitor picked you out. Like he did me. He must be recruiting other fairies to join the hunters. The question was, why?

"It's not that odd," said Erin. "I mean, it doesn't sound like fairies care much for picking up their half-human offspring. Um, I don't mean you, Blair. I know your dad's in jail and it's not really his fault he can't visit."

I averted my gaze, far from in the mood to talk about my dad after the turmoil of emotions the market had already kicked off inside me. "I guess they have to put strong glamours on their half-human kids, or they'd be flying around the human world terrifying everyone."

"You, terrifying?" Erin snorted. "Even Buck's like a cuddly bunny rabbit compared to the Inquisitor."

Ice slid down my spine. My throat tightened, and while I wanted to admit what I knew, I didn't dare. Even telling Alissa had been risky, and in the end, knowing the man who led the hunters was a fairy hadn't changed anything.

If *he* had the Pixie-Glass, my last hope of contacting my dad had just gone up in a shower of pixie dust.

———

"Any luck?" Nathan asked, when I met him at the pub later.

I sat down at our usual table, but even the comforting warmth and cheery atmosphere didn't raise my spirits. "I asked about the Pixie-Glass, and apparently Blythe's mother of all people was the last person known to be looking for one at the market. Years ago."

His eyes went wide. "Seriously?"

"Yep." I listlessly tapped on the menu to order my food, not really having much of an appetite. "So, not only am I without a way to contact my dad, it wouldn't surprise me if the hunters seized the Pixie-Glass when they arrested Mrs Dailey last year. I don't know who got all her possessions."

I doubted she'd have given them to either of her children, but who did that leave? Maybe I should ask Rebecca during our next lesson. As for Blythe, she didn't even live in Fairy Falls anymore. She'd lost her job at Dritch & Co after she'd tried to bully me into leaving town, and while we weren't exactly mortal enemies anymore, she and I hadn't parted on pleasant terms either. Mostly, I'd been in shock when she'd told me the hunters' leader wasn't human. But she couldn't have moved too far away from town, since she kept in contact with her sister.

"What about the guy in the hospital?" Nathan asked. "Any luck finding out how he got here?"

"Not really." I exhaled in a sigh. "If it was goblin brew he drank, it ought to have worn off after twenty-four hours. Either someone's smuggling him more of the stuff under the table or it's not that at all, but the goblins weren't exactly keen to talk to me about it. They thought the elf was flinging the blame at them on purpose. Elves and goblins don't get along."

"Yes, I can see how they might have that impression," Nathan said. "Do you think the goblins were innocent, Blair?"

"Not a word I'd use." I looked down at the table, thinking of those dancing, bewitched humans. "But I don't think they did it, no. The market seems to exist outside of the usual paranormal rules, though, so it'd be hard to convict them if it turned out one of them did it."

His mouth pressed into a line. "Yes, I know. Steve wouldn't touch a case like that no matter what you offered him."

"So I take it he's thrilled the market's coming here next week?"

"Ecstatic." He picked up his fork when our food appeared on the table. "He spent half our meeting ranting about how the guy in our hospital is none of our business whatsoever and we should kick him out of town. I had to give him a lecture on basic paranormal laws."

I rolled my eyes, feeling a little better now I had the mental image of Steve getting a major schooling. "Anyone would think he hadn't been the head of the town's police force for the last few years. Did he even read the handbook?"

He grinned. "Do you really want me to answer that question?"

"Hey, I've just had a dismal failure of a day. Please tell me all the stories you have of Steve acting the fool."

"I can do one better," he said. "Would it improve your mood if I said I'm not on the night shift, and you're welcome to stay over at mine?"

"You bet." My family life might be a disaster, but at least my romantic life was going well. Better than I'd ever hoped it would.

My phone buzzed in my bag. I pulled it out to find a message from my foster mum, wanting to know if Nathan and I were definitely free at the weekend.

"Something up?" Nathan gave me a questioning look.

"I was supposed to call my foster parents and confirm our plans for the weekend, but I haven't had a moment to spare all day." My finger hesitated over the touch screen. "Once I confirm this, there's no going back."

Nathan laughed. "Blair, I'm pretty sure it isn't going to be that bad."

He was right. My foster parents were a harmless retired couple with no ties to the hunters and no reason to react to Nathan the way his own family had reacted to me. What could possibly go wrong?

Famous last words, Blair.

5

I woke the following morning to the sound of someone tapping on the window. It took me a confused moment to remember I was at Nathan's house, so nobody should be able to reach the window from the ground.

"Miaow," said Sky, in disgruntled tones.

Next to him, Nathan didn't stir, and I didn't have the heart to wake him up. Another tapping noise sounded, and I padded over to the window. I'd expected to see the pixie hovering outside, but instead, a small pointed-eared man wearing brown-green clothes stood in the bushes below. An elf. Bramble lifted another stone and threw it at the window, where it bounced off with a ringing noise.

All right, I'm coming.

I grabbed my slippers and dressing gown and made my way downstairs to the hall. It was freezing at this hour, but the elf wore his usual threadbare clothing and didn't seem bothered by the frost dusting the grass on Nathan's front lawn.

"Oh, hello, Bramble." I leaned on the door frame to speak to him. "Is something wrong?"

"I heard about the human," he said.

My heart missed a beat. "You mean Riff, the normal? How'd you know?"

"People talk, Blair Wilkes," he said. "They know you went to the market. You must tread with caution."

"What's the issue?" I screwed my forehead up, too tired to deal with cryptic elf rambling this early in the morning. "I've never had the chance to meet any other fairies before, and besides, we had to find out what happened to the normal—"

"It is not safe to speak of such things here," he interrupted. "You must come to the king's domain."

I glanced behind me, but it didn't sound like Nathan was awake yet. The elf king had an annoying habit of presenting more questions than answers, but he'd eventually given me enough hints to be able to piece together what'd happened to my father before his arrest.

"Okay, I'll come to see the king," I said. "Once I get some proper clothes on and tell Nathan where I'm going."

It wasn't my first morning excursion into the woods, but when Nathan didn't wake even when I went back into his room to get dressed. Sky had already happily fallen asleep in my spot on the bed, so I scribbled a note telling Nathan where I was in case he woke up, and texted Alissa telling her the same.

After closing the door behind me, I followed the elf through the quiet streets until we reached the entrance to the forest.

Inside, a thick layer of fog hung over the trees, and my breath clouded the air as I walked. The forest covered the north side of town, extending around the edges of the lake, but it felt endless when I reached the part where no signs of human habitation were visible through the thick trees. The elf walked in silence along paths which wove through ancient oaks and around tangled undergrowth. Even after several visits, I would have got lost if I'd been alone, and it didn't help that the forest looked different in winter. While bright flowers had once filled the surrounding area, they remained dead and withered, the carpet of leaves covered in frost. The sound of birdsong came from the gnarled trees bordering the paths, and to my surprise, I found myself missing the pixie who'd sometimes accompanied me here.

Did the hunters catch him visiting my dad? Is that why he disappeared?

The elves' king lived inside a giant hollow tree with sprawling roots extending across the forest floor. In the surrounding bushes stood countless elves dressed in green and brown, wielding sharpened branches like spears. They knew who I was by now, so they let me pass without a fuss. As I did so, I snapped my fingers to undo my glamour, bringing out my wings.

Not that it made it any easier to get into the elves' tunnel, which was built for people a foot shorter than me. As usual, I had to walk at a crouch through the narrow passageway until it widened into a cave.

Inside, the elf king sat in the centre on a tree stump carved into the likeness of a throne. He wore clothes patterned with gold leaves and a crown on his head. I bent into an awkward bow, conscious of the mud on my knees from crawling in the tunnel.

"Blair Wilkes," said the elf king. "It has been some time

since we last spoke."

"It has." The king might look human, but he wasn't, and was quick to take offence. I had to tread with caution if I wanted to gain the answers I needed. "Is there a reason you wanted to speak with me?"

"A human was found wandering around under the effects of a spell," he said. "That human is still here in Fairy Falls."

"Yes," I said. "He is, but we can't let him leave until we find out how to undo the spell he's under. We don't want any other normals to end up affected, too."

"Yes, we must maintain our secrecy," said the elf king. "That is why you must investigate the goblin market and find the person who is enacting trickery on humans."

My mouth parted in surprise. "I was at the market yesterday and I tried asking questions, but nobody there knew how the human came to be under a spell. They weren't lying, either."

The elf king looked down at me with an unreadable expression on his pointed face. "The goblins are well practised in the act of deceit, and if they are bewitching humans without consequence, it will spell bad news for all of our kind."

"I know, but I didn't find any conclusive evidence that they might be responsible," I said. "Madame Grey has taken on responsibility for the normal as long as he's in the hospital, but until the spell wears off, we can only guess how he ended up in that state."

"Precisely why you must take it upon yourself to learn the source of the trickery," he said firmly. "You have your feet in two worlds, which gives you a unique insight."

"Um, I wouldn't say it does," I said. "The fairies at the

market weren't all that keen to speak to me. They saw me as a human."

"They did," he said, "which is why you must convince them otherwise."

I frowned. "You mean go in as a fairy."

Maybe that's why they'd been so disdainful towards me. I'd been wearing my glamour while I'd spoken to them and they'd seen me as an outsider. But would that really change if I got out my wings?

"Exactly," said the elf king.

I wasn't convinced. Fairy or human, I was still a newbie to that side of the magical world, and if someone at the market had bewitched that poor human, it seemed unlikely that the fairies would tell tales on one another to a stranger.

On the other hand, if I showed them I *wanted* to learn more about the fairies, perhaps I'd have a better shot at finding answers about the Pixie-Glass.

"Even if I did that, the laws of Fairy Falls don't cover the market," I said. "It sounds like Steve doesn't want to know. So even if I managed to find who did it, I wouldn't be able to hand them over to the authorities."

I debated asking him if he'd sent one of his people to snoop around as the goblins had claimed, but that probably wasn't a wise idea.

"Yes, the laws of the market are self-contained," he growled. "However, someone lured the human into the market to begin with, and *that* is grounds for punishment with the weight of the magical laws."

"So I have to find who invited him in? As opposed to who gave him the drink?"

That seemed a tall order. There'd been dozens of

people at the market, and they probably attracted a new crowd every day.

"It should not be difficult," said Bramble. "The goblins are known for their trickery and cannot resist bragging of their accomplishments to one another."

"I heard elves and goblins aren't traditionally the best of friends," I said. "Um, not that I'm accusing you of anything, but there's an elf in the hospital called Thistle who's a known troublemaker. He's the one who sent me to the market, and the other day, he was nearly arrested for exposing our world to normals. Doesn't that make him likely to be responsible for tricking a normal?"

"I know of that elf," said Bramble. "A fool, but not one who intends harm."

I had my doubts, but it was possible that the elves knew perfectly well that he was more likely to be the culprit and were too stubborn to admit it. Then again, the goblins hadn't exactly seemed concerned about the consequences for anyone who ended up drinking their magical brews.

"Might he have brought the goblin brew with him into the town?" I pressed. "He might have given it to the human himself without him ever having to enter the market."

"Whether he did or not, you are to find answers, Blair Wilkes," said the elf king. "I must stress that this is not just important for all of us, but for the sake of your people, too."

"You mean..." I faltered. "You think people might blame the fairies?"

The slight problem with that was that I was the only fairy in town. Aside from Buck, but he didn't live in Fairy

Falls, and besides, few people knew what he was. He hadn't interacted with the fairies at the market either. But then, not much was at stake for him. He'd never met his fairy parent, let alone communicated with them behind bars like I had.

"They might blame all of us, Blair," he said. "Many do not trust the fae, with good reason."

I thought back to the kindly fairy man I'd met. He hadn't seemed as unfriendly as the two women had, but could I really tell anything from one interaction? "All right, I'll go back to the market and ask around. And… can I ask you a question?"

"A favour, Blair Wilkes?" asked the elf king.

"Not a favour," I said. "I just wondered—have you ever heard of a Pixie-Glass?"

His expression was blank. "I've heard the word, yes, but I have never encountered such a thing."

True. If the elves hadn't heard of it, it might be a fairy-only thing. Or as rare as the fairies at the market claimed. Just my luck for my dad to send me after something impossible to find.

A rush of reckless daring seized me. "My dad mentioned it, so I wondered if he might have said anything while he was here in the forest."

Years back, my dad had spent time here among the elf king's domain. That was the reason the elves had contacted me to start with, though our weird mutual understanding had evolved over time.

"No," said the elf king. "He didn't. Is that all, Blair Wilkes?"

"Just one more question." I drew in a breath. "Did you know the hunters recruited fairies?"

The elven king gave me an appraising look. "What gives you that impression?"

"I met one." I tried to ignore the way my heart kicked against my ribs. While the elves weren't as fond of spreading gossip as, say, the witches or the werewolves, speaking the truth seemed to make the Inquisitor's presence feel closer than before. "A hunter. He was personally recruited."

"We have heard… rumours," said the king, with a glance at Bramble. "Rumours of the dangerous individual who leads the hunters. We have never met this man, but he is no friend to us."

Considering you helped my dad… I guess not. Not that they'd really known what they were getting themselves into at the time. One winter, several years ago, my dad had appeared in the woods and found himself trespassing on the elves' territory. He'd begged them for shelter, as he was fleeing for his life, and they'd let him stay, not knowing who it was he fled from.

Now, I was almost certain that the fairies he'd been fleeing and the hunters who'd caught and jailed him had been one and the same.

"I don't understand," I murmured, half to myself. "Why would fairies hunt other paranormals?"

"Who can say?" said Bramble. "You'll have to ask another fairy, one who's lived in their realm. We do things differently here."

No kidding. Despite all the answers the elves had given me, I remained as much in the dark about the fairies as ever. But I hadn't given up on the market yet. Maybe I did need to go in there as a fairy, and convince the others that I belonged among them, if I wanted the truth.

———

I left the forest to find a message from Nathan saying he'd found my note and left for work, so I headed back home instead. I walked into the flat to find Alissa had made us both coffee, which was welcome after trekking in the forest in the cold. Sky, in typical cat fashion, had already wandered back here from Nathan's house and stolen my place on the sofa.

I went to change into my work clothes before joining Alissa in the living room.

"The elves?" she said. "It's been a while, hasn't it? Let me guess… they want a favour from you."

"You've got it." I picked up my coffee mug, savouring the warmth. "The elves want me to find the person responsible for giving the goblin brew to that normal. They hinted that the fairies in general might take the blame otherwise. So I have to go back to the market and snoop around as a fairy rather than a witch this time."

I'd told Alissa about yesterday's events before I'd gone to meet Nathan at the pub, and she'd listened with wide eyes as I recounted my misadventures at the market. I'd hesitated before telling her about the two fairies I'd run into, a fresh wave of shame washing over me at the memory. Nathan had been kind about it, but neither he nor Alissa could fully understand the nature of my relationship to the fairies. I didn't understand it myself, most of the time.

"When the market arrives in Fairy Falls, it'll be easier to figure out who's likely to have made trouble," Alissa said. "Did anyone strike you as acting suspiciously?"

"The goblins." I took a long sip of coffee. "But then

again, the elves and goblins are rivals, so it's entirely possible the elves are trying to get the goblins into trouble. I think Thistle looks more guilty than they do, to be honest. How is he, anyway?"

"Stubbornly denying knowing Riff at all," she said. "Personally, I can't wait for him to be discharged, but no doubt he'll go running back to the market as soon as it reaches Fairy Falls and end up half-drowned in the lake or something."

"Wouldn't surprise me," I said. "So—is Riff still staying in the town hospital?"

"We don't have a choice but to keep him here until he can tell us who he is and where he came from." Her gaze dropped. "It's not ideal, but right now, he's the only person who might be able to help us prevent whoever brought him here from targeting other normals. These things are rarely a one-off."

"It's got to be more than goblin brew," I said. "If it's lasted this long. And if someone lured him into the market on purpose, perhaps they might do it again."

"Exactly," she said. "The security team should be able to prevent any more incidents once the market reaches town, though. My grandmother will keep an eye out for trouble, but she always has her hands full at this time of year."

"I'll be at work when the market shows up." Then again, Veronica seemed keen for us to recruit local businesses to get involved in the market. And they'd need help setting everything up when they arrived in town. Maybe I could convince her to get Dritch & Co involved, too. It had to be worth a try, right?

Once I had a spare moment at work, I knocked on Veronica's office door.

"Come in!" she said in a singsong voice. She was in a good mood. That should make her easier to convince, I hoped.

I entered her office and had to screw up my eyes against the explosion of bright lights. Disco balls floated on the ceiling, at least five of them, each in a different neon shade. Veronica's office changed décor depending on her mood, and right now, I guessed she was either bored or happy. Given the way she swivelled on her rotating chair, I'd guess the former.

She spun to face me. "Something you wanted to ask me, Blair?"

"Yeah." I kept my eyes on her face to avoid half-blinding myself. "I know we've asked a bunch of local businesses to join the market when it arrives in town, but I wondered how the owners of the market would feel about some of us helping them set up. They've travelled a long way, so I think they'd appreciate it."

"Some of us?" she said. "Who?"

"Uh. Me." I tripped over my words. "I wanted to volunteer to help out. I thought it'd give a great first impression of Fairy Falls, and we might be able to get them interested in hiring us in the future."

My speech had sounded better in my head, but I'd said the magic words. Veronica beamed. "Yes, that's an excellent idea. I'll make a couple of calls. Blair, you should let the others know. I'm sure my daughter would love to help, too."

"Uh, I haven't talked to Bethan about it—"

"You can take business cards with you and hand them out," she went on. "I'll ask Lizzie to print more fliers, and we'll set up a proper stall for Dritch & Co. I'm sure the others won't mind giving you a hand, too."

Uh-oh. Bethan and the others wouldn't be thrilled at me volunteering them for extra work. "We don't all have to," I said quickly. "I just had an idea about helping out, but—"

"Opportunities like this don't come along every day, Blair." She rotated on her swivel chair and rose to her feet. "Tell the others, won't you? I'll be right behind you."

What have I got myself into?

———

"You did what?" asked Bethan.

"We'll be helping set up the market tomorrow," said Veronica, clapping her hands at us and making the printer let out a squawk of alarm. "I thought it would be good for the town's reputation. Blair, thank you for suggesting it."

Everyone looked at me, and a flush crept up my neck. Veronica, meanwhile, walked around the office giving orders to the others. "So, we'll need fifty business cards… make it a hundred. No, five hundred."

Lizzie blinked at the boss. "Are you expecting that many people to be interested in hiring us? Don't forget everyone in town already knows who we are."

"Because we're notorious," Rob put in cheerfully.

"And it's time to capitalise on that reputation," the boss said, sailing out of the office and letting the door swing shut behind her.

"Blair." Bethan's brow pinched. "What in the world did you do?"

"I volunteered to help with setting up the market," I said guiltily. "I didn't realise she'd rope the whole office into turning it into a marketing opportunity."

"*Why?*" she asked. "Don't get me wrong, it's a break from sitting in a stuffy office all day, but it's freezing out there."

"I'll make hot cocoa for all of us," said Rob, ever the optimist. "It'll be fun."

"Uh-huh." Lizzie switched on the printer. "If you think standing outside in the rain handing out fliers is fun."

"The others at the market might give us freebies for helping out," said Rob. "I'm told goblin brew rivals werewolf cocktails for potency. Want to try it, Blair?"

"No thanks." I shuddered. "Didn't you hear about the normal who wandered into Fairy Falls the other day? We think he ended up under the influence of something he got at the market. Madame Grey does, anyway."

"So you're volunteering us to play detective?" said Bethan.

"I volunteered myself," I said. "I shouldn't have said anything, but I couldn't think of a better idea to get behind the scenes at the market and find out who might want to trick an unsuspecting human into falling under their spell."

Bethan arched a brow. "You didn't expect my mother to run away with your idea? It'll be lucky if she doesn't have us standing out there dressed as Dritch & Co's mascots."

6

By the end of the workday, my second thoughts about my plan had become third and fourth thoughts, and I was starting to wish I'd just opted to visit the market after work tomorrow instead.

After I left work, I headed to the hospital on the way to my magic lesson. Despite the elf king's insistence that the goblins had something to hide, I was inclined to believe Thistle was far from innocent in our visitor's plight. Alissa wouldn't be working today, but the elf would be even harder to get hold of once he'd been discharged, so I had to waylay him before then.

I pushed open the doors and entered the hospital lobby, finding it empty. Maybe I should have waited until after my magic lesson instead.

"Hello," said a voice, causing me to jump violently. Old Ava poked her head out from behind a potted plant. The old seer hadn't dropped her habit of being unpredictable, it seemed.

"Uh… hi," I said. "Are you supposed to be out of your room?"

Based on past experience, I'd say no. The elderly witch sidled into view, her purple wig in disarray and her wand tucked behind her ear. The wand was only a prop, not a real wand—which, given her tendency to threaten to hex the hospital staff on a regular basis, was probably for the best.

"You don't look sick," she said. "What are you doing here?"

"I'm looking for an elf," I said, deciding there was no harm in telling the truth. "Have you seen Thistle? I need to speak to him."

"Mischief is afoot," she said. "I saw it. Mischief, and fairy wings."

"Ava, how did you sneak out of your room?" Lou, the Asian woman who worked with Alissa, walked into the waiting room and shook her head at the old witch. "Oh, hey, Blair. Did you need something?"

"I wondered if I could have a word with Thistle," I said. "If he's still here, that is."

"He's refusing to take a healing spell for his broken bones, so yes, he is," she said. "We confiscated his bottles of alcohol, so he's in a foul mood. Fair warning."

"He had alcohol in here?" I dropped my voice. "I don't know if Alissa told you, but we think Riff might be under the influence of goblin brew, from the market. Same as him."

"Oh, it wasn't goblin brew that Thistle was drinking," she said, wrinkling her nose. "It was one of those awful cocktails he likes. Anyway, you can speak to him, but I can't promise he'll be in a cooperative mood."

With a nod of thanks, I followed her directions to the ward. The elf sat up in bed, looking very sorry for himself.

"Hello," said Thistle. "Come to have a good laugh, have you?"

"Not at all," I said. "I wanted to ask you a couple of questions."

"If you want to know if I've ever seen that fine gentleman next door before he arrived here, I can't say I have."

True. As far as the elf was concerned, poor Riff was a stranger to him. It was worth a shot, though.

"Did you see anyone else from Fairy Falls at the market when you went?" I pressed on.

"The girl who makes those lovely cocktails was there, buying supplies," he said, in wistful tones. "Delightful girl. Great talent."

"Who is she?" I asked.

"Pix, she calls herself. She works at the Laughing Pixie."

The Laughing Pixie was a bit of a dump, but it was popular with students for its Happy Hour discounts. The elf was a little old for that crowd, but if this Pix had been shopping at the market, maybe she'd seen something when she'd been there.

"Thanks," I said, backing out of the room.

"You're late, Briar," said old Ava from behind my shoulder. For the second time that day, I nearly jumped out of my skin. "Very late."

"Late for what?" My gaze caught on the clock on the waiting room wall. Oh, no. I was running late for my magic lesson.

I hurried out of the hospital and switched on my levitating boots, but I was still ten minutes late when I burst into the classroom to find Rebecca already sitting there with her textbook open on her desk. Her fluffy orange cat familar, Toast, curled up behind her seat.

"Blair," said Rita. "I was beginning to wonder if you would come."

"Sorry, I've been run off my feet at work," I said breathlessly. "Preparing for the market."

"I see," she said, her tone indicating she didn't believe me. "You'll be doing theory work today. Get out your textbook and turn to page two hundred and twenty."

I sat down and got out my textbook, my cheeks burning. The newly repaired wall was enough proof that it was for the best that we skipped practical training today, though I didn't fare much better at remembering dates and facts. My mind was elsewhere, and it came as a relief to be dismissed, even if Rita did give us a heap of homework.

After the lesson was over, I dithered over gathering my things to leave the classroom, then tailed Rebecca outside until we were far enough from the classroom that Rita wouldn't overhear us. "Is your sister around?"

"My sister?" Her brow furrowed. "No. Why?"

"I have a question I want to ask her, but I didn't want to distract you from your lessons. It's about… your mum."

She stiffened. "Ask me. I might know."

"All right," I said. "Did your mum ever mention owning a Pixie-Glass?"

She blinked. "A what?"

Worth a shot. It was too much to hope that Mrs Dailey had dropped any hints in front of her younger daughter.

She might have told Blythe, but she wasn't in town as far as I knew.

"It's something I'm looking for," I said vaguely. "I heard a rumour your mum was looking for one years ago. But she might not have it anymore, anyway."

"I'll ask my sister."

"Ah—you don't have to do that," I said hastily. "I'll speak to her next time I see her. It's not urgent."

I *hoped* it wasn't, but Mrs Dailey was the only lead I had, and if she'd ever owned a Pixie-Glass, the odds of it being anywhere other than in the hunters' hands were depressingly low.

No, I was better off concentrating on tracking down who'd bewitched Riff, before I ended up in hot water myself.

Firstly, I had to find this Pix person, which meant heading to the Laughing Pixie. In my book, the student pub was only marginally more bearable than the New Moon, the haunt of the werewolf pack's notorious band. Crowds of students filled every table, drinking cheap pints and neon-coloured cocktails from grimy glasses. Trying to ignore the way my shoes stuck to the floor with every step, I made my way over to the bar, where a vaguely familiar girl was polishing a glass with a cloth. *What was her name again?* Clare. The former assistant to the town's spell-maker, before his untimely death.

"Excuse me?" What with the noise, I had to lean over the bar and more or less shout in her face. "Clare?"

She looked up. "I know you. Blair, right?"

"Yeah," I said. "I wondered if Pix was in. She makes cocktails, right?"

"Sure, she's in the back." She turned around and called over her shoulder, "Pix, someone wants to speak to you."

A young woman entered the bar. About twenty or so, she had bright pink spiky hair and wore glasses decorated with miniature unicorns. Her apron was covered with bright stains, while she carried a cocktail glass in one hand.

"Hey," she said. "Looking for a cocktail special? Happy Hour doesn't begin till six, but as a new customer, I can brew you up a pink swirl-a-thon that'll make your eyes sparkle."

"No, thanks." Fairy glitter was more than enough without adding sparkling eyes on top of it. "I'm looking into an incident involving the goblin market, and I'm told you went there earlier this week."

Her smile vanished. "What incident?"

"I don't know if you heard, but a human—a normal—showed up in town recently under the influence of an intoxicating substance," I explained. "We have reason to believe it happened at the market, so I'm speaking to everyone who went there. Thistle told me you buy cocktail supplies from the market when it's around."

"That scoundrel." She put down the glass. "Yes, I do buy from the markets when I can. They carry ingredients which are hard to get hold of elsewhere."

"Like what?" I asked. "Goblin brew?"

"Who'd put that in a cocktail? It's strong enough on its own." She gave a theatrical shudder. "If you're thinking of trying it, Blair, don't."

Hmm. "What's it made of?"

"The main ingredient is a potent and rare plant called

goblin fruit," said Pix. "They say it causes hallucinations if consumed directly."

"So can the goblin fruit have the same effect as the brew?" I asked.

"Of course it can," said Pix. "Worse, if anything, because it's undiluted. Nasty stuff."

Might Riff have consumed goblin fruit? It'd explain why the effects had lasted longer than they should have. But that didn't mean the elf wasn't involved in his plight.

"Did you see anyone else from town at the market?" I asked. "From Fairy Falls, I mean?"

Her forehead scrunched up. "Argyle Winthrop was there. She's a gardener witch. Works at the local herb shop."

"All right," I said. "Thank you."

It was already getting late by the time I headed down the high street towards the herb shop, and I found the place closed for the night. It was a pretty run-down shop, with roof tiles missing and the windows boarded up, but a light in the upstairs window confirmed someone lived up there.

I'd have to drop by after work tomorrow—assuming Veronica didn't make us stay at the market from morning until evening, handing out fliers. *That really wasn't your best idea, Blair.*

———

While part of me clung onto the slim hope that Veronica would have changed her mind by morning, luck wasn't on my side. Mid-morning, the entire office of Dritch & Co set off for the market—minus Callie, who seemed positively cheerful at being left inside to sit at the front desk while the rest of us trekked through the hills in the cold drizzle.

I'd anticipated our day to involve a lot of packing and carrying boxes across the countryside, but instead, we arrived in a deserted field to find the market was just… there. As though it'd transported itself across the countryside of its own accord. Which, in all probability, was exactly how it had reached town. I tried to ignore the others' disgruntled looks, knowing the boss had doubtless come up with a backup plan.

Sure enough, Veronica wasted no time in conjuring up a stall with 'Dritch & Co' emblazoned across it in neon letters and setting Lizzie and me to work handing out flyers to anyone who passed. Meanwhile, Bethan and Rob walked among the crowd doing the same, underneath a giant umbrella with the same design as our stall.

"I suppose we should thank our lucky stars she *didn't* put us in costumes," I remarked, handing a leaflet to a group of goblins. "You did a great job making the leaflets, by the way."

"Best I could do on short-notice," said Lizzie. "To be honest, I wouldn't mind putting on a disguise so nobody from town recognises us. I mean, just look at the boss."

Veronica stood among a group of elves, talking animatedly. Her own umbrella was bright pink, decorated with fairy wings. I suppressed a groan. "Next she'll make me get *my* wings out."

That's what I got for taking the initiative. Admittedly, the wings would be handy when it came to questioning the fairies, but I'd rather not take off my glamour and flit about in front of all my colleagues. I tried listening to the goblins' conversations whenever a group of them passed, but I heard nothing that might implicate anyone here at the market in the crime of handing goblin fruit over to normals.

Soon enough, the town's citizens began to trickle into the market, drawn by the noise. Some set up their own stalls, while the general public formed a steady flow of traffic from one end of the market to the other. Lizzie and I stood side by side, offering flyers to anyone who passed.

"The people who work here already *have* employment," I muttered to Lizzie through chattering teeth. "What does Veronica think she's accomplishing with this?"

"I think she's hoping they'll take the business cards and distribute them across every town the market visits," she said, handing a leaflet to a passing goblin. "Not a bad strategy, really."

Rob walked past our stall, helping the goblins carry a giant barrel to the 'goblin brew' stall. "How'd he get that?"

"Probably charmed them into letting him help out," said Lizzie.

I watched Rob carry the barrel out of sight, making a mental note to ask him if he'd taken note of anything amiss as soon as Veronica dismissed us. For all I knew, the barrel was overflowing with illegal goblin fruit, while I was stuck here handing out fliers.

I was shuffling from one foot to another to keep warm when I spotted a small black cat walking through the market. A cat with one white paw. "Sky, where did you come from?"

"Miaow," he said.

Another faint mew followed. My mouth dropped

open. A group of small cats gathered behind Sky, following his lead. Each of them was smaller than a regular cat, more kitten-sized, but had the same oddly coloured eyes and regal air. Even their mewing sounded different to regular cats.

Fairy cats. A whole congregation of fairy cats had found Sky. Or rather, he'd found them. From the way they followed his lead, he'd already established himself as the leader of the group. Honestly. My cat had been at the market for all of five minutes and he'd already gained a throng of worshippers. Maybe I needed to ask him for tips.

———

After Veronica finally let us go for the day, I briefly left the market to stop by the gardener's shop to look for Argyle Winthrop, only to find the place closed early on Fridays. Resigned, I prepared to return home to get backup before I went back to do some more questioning, then hesitated. If I took Alissa or Nathan with me to the market, I'd never be able to get away with pretending to be more of a fairy than a witch. Assuming the fairies hadn't already seen me handing out flyers on behalf of an eccentric witch who carried an umbrella decorated with fairy wings all day, that is.

Half the town seemed to be on their way to the market, as I discovered when I joined the crowd flowing back to the field, following the sound of laughter and music and general merriment. Taking in a deep breath, I snapped my fingers and turned into my fairy self. I held my head high, determined to ignore the stares.

If I had to go in as a witch undercover, so be it.

By now, the market was in full swing. The band had set up their stage between two trees and were already surrounded by a dancing crowd, but I couldn't tell if any of the dancers were normal humans or if everyone was magical. Despite all the security around the area, the market carried an otherworldly air, like it lay somewhere apart from the rest of the world. Even with my fairy wings out, I had the distinct impression that I'd stepped onto another planet in which the regular rules no longer applied.

I beat my wings, hovering on the spot until I located the costume stall staffed by the same two fairies as last time. When I flew over to greet them, they both raised their eyebrows at the sight of my wings.

"So it's true," said the blond fairy.

"That I'm a fairy?" I said. "Yes. Is the man I spoke to yesterday around?"

"Dill?" said her companion. "He'll be here somewhere."

I scanned the crowd, but there were so many faces, new and old, ranging from humans to elves to various others I'd never seen before. Witches shopping for charms or buying rare ingredients, elves catching up with old friends, goblins enticing customers to buy their wares—and endless cups of that infamous goblin brew. I turned back to the two fairies to avoid getting distracted by the shiny newness of the market. I'd come here for a reason.

"Can I ask you a question?" I said. "Fairy Falls—it was founded by fairies, right? So why aren't they around anymore?"

"*You're* around," said the blond fairy.

"I know I am, but I didn't grow up here," I explained.

"I'm the first fairy to move to town in years. Why'd they leave?"

She shrugged. "I'm not that old. I heard it was centuries ago that they left."

Centuries. That fit with what I'd heard since I'd moved here, but were any fairies old enough to remember that time? The books I'd read on the subject said that it was rumoured the original fairies were immortal, but I wasn't sure how much truth there was in that statement.

"Listen, if you want to learn more about us, we're free for a couple of hours tomorrow," the brunette fairy said. "We have a break around three. Look for us then. I assume you're going to be around, right?"

"Oh—sure," I said. "What's your name? I'm Blair."

"I'm Holly," said the blond fairy.

"And I'm Heather," added the other.

Tomorrow. That was after my foster parents' visit… which I was also woefully unprepared for. I'd been too distracted by everything else to really think about it.

"Okay, thanks." I turned away as a muscular blond man walked past the stall. Rob. I waylaid him before he disappeared into the crowd. "There you are. What were you helping the goblins carry earlier?"

"Just more of their brew," he said. "They can't make it fresh, because the ingredients are rare. That's what they told me, anyway. Nice guys, if a little mischievous."

"By ingredients, do you mean goblin fruit?"

"I dunno, you'll have to ask them." He pointed towards their stall, which was overflowing with endless mugs of goblin brew like the previous evening. "By the way, I like your wings."

Oops. I was supposed to be playing fairy, not talking

to my werewolf colleague. I said goodbye and made my way to the goblins' stall. This time, only one goblin sat there, and he gave me a frown when he spotted me.

"You look different," he observed.

"Decided to come here as a fairy this time," I told him. "I don't suppose you've seen a witch called Argyle Winthrop here at the market?"

I figured I'd start with the other people from Fairy Falls before questioning anyone else at the market.

"Never heard of her," he said. "Lots of people come here. Some stay, some go, and we let them. This is a safe place for people like us."

People like us. My heart sank a little. By accusing anyone at the market of bewitching humans without proof, I'd be making life more difficult for the others who'd done nothing wrong. No wonder he'd rightfully treated me like a human and not a fairy.

"Do you sell anything except for goblin brew?" I asked.

"Why would I?" he said. "Maybe after a cup or three, your senses might be sharp enough to find what you're looking for. Like them."

My gaze followed where he pointed, towards the crowd gathering among the stalls. Almost all of them carried a mug of goblin brew. It couldn't be harmful if everyone here was drinking it, right? It was supposed to have a stronger effect on humans than fairies, besides, and perhaps after a drink or two, I'd feel more comfortable mingling with the crowd. And maybe people might be more likely to talk to me if I looked as though I belonged here.

The goblin held out a mug of the brew, and the intoxicating scent filled my nostrils.

"It won't transform me into a toadstool or anything?" I asked.

"Not unless you drink the entire barrel." He bared his teeth in a grin. "For humans, one cup is enough to make them forget their own names, but us fair folk are made of stronger stuff."

True. Not a word he'd said was a lie, so I handed over the cash for a mug of goblin brew. Despite its unappealing appearance, the brew tasted as sweet as it smelled, and after a sip or two, I did feel less like a child lost in a supermarket.

"I'm told goblin fruit is stronger," I said to the goblin. "Does anyone sell that here?"

"Goblin fruit?" He hooted with laughter. "No. It spoils too easily. We make the brew when we're not on the road."

True. He was telling the truth, as far as he knew, but perhaps someone else here might have a different story to tell. The fruit to make the goblin brew had to come from somewhere, after all.

I walked away from the stall and wove through the crowd. From the sheer volume of people around me, not everyone here had come from Fairy Falls. Everyone looked paranormal, though, and my senses didn't pick up on anyone out of place. Most of the fairies were dancing in front of the band, their bright wings fluttering. Not a good place for me to try asking them questions, so I stayed among the stalls, drinking my goblin brew in the hope that I'd eventually stop feeling out of place.

My gaze fell on a stall on my right, selling various potted plants. Behind it stood a female goblin with longer hair than the others I'd seen, wearing a dress made of dandelions.

"Hey," I said to the female goblin. "I don't suppose you sell goblin fruit?"

"Who wants to know?" she said. "We're perfectly legal, we are."

"I'm not saying you aren't," I said hastily, "but a man recently stumbled into Fairy Falls who shouldn't have known about the paranormal world. We think someone gave him goblin fruit, so I just wondered if someone had bought any….?"

"No," she said. "We only sell seedlings, and they take a long while to grow. No fruit here."

"Did you sell any seedlings to someone from Fairy Falls?" I asked.

"We don't ask where anyone comes from," she said. "This is a safe place."

I kept hearing that. And I wanted it to stay safe, for the sake of the other fairies. At least the goblin brew dulled my frustration. The music seemed to be growing louder, faster, more insistent, vibrating in my bones. No matter how far I walked, I couldn't escape the rhythm. Finally, I gave in and let my wings stretch out the way they wanted to, beating behind my shoulders in a way that felt more natural than walking on two feet.

Next thing I knew, I'd found my way to the dance floor, or maybe the dance floor had found me. The sound of the music and the beat of my feet and my wings overwhelmed everything else, and the fairies' laughter and music swept me into a whirling circle.

After a while, I was vaguely aware of someone tugging on my arm. Buck's face swam before mine, strange to my newly altered eyes. Wings poked out of his shoulders, while his face was shinier and pointier than usual. I smiled and tried to pull him into the group dance, but he tugged me out of line, yelling something in my ear. I heard the word 'Nathan'.

Then I saw Nathan himself, standing behind Buck with a concerned expression on his face. He caught my hand in his, dragging me out of the dance. I heard exclamations of disappointment from behind me.

"It's okay, he's with me!" I tried to say, but nothing came out but a slurred jumble.

Nathan tightened my grip on his hand as I fell against him, the world lurching sideways. The ground's tilt made me stagger into his arms, and all went black.

7

The next morning, I was pretty sure I was dead. Or dying. The instant my eyes opened, I flew to the bathroom to throw up. Then I lay on the floor for a bit, vaguely aware that I was still in my fairy form and couldn't even lie down comfortably.

Even werewolf cocktail hangovers had nothing on this. I pushed to my feet and staggered out of the room, hanging onto the door as though I'd fall into empty space if I let go.

"Blair!" Alissa appeared in front of me, concerned. "Are you okay?"

"I think I'm dying."

"What did you drink?" she asked. "You look worse than Lou after a night at the cocktail bar."

"Goblin brew." I pushed myself upright, my head pounding. "It's evil, evil stuff. No wonder that poor Riff guy is still a mess."

"Actually, he's ready to be discharged today," she said. "I was going to tell you after work yesterday, but you disappeared in the market and I didn't know where you'd gone until Nathan brought you home."

I groaned. "Just great."

"It's good news," Alissa said. "Riff remembers who he is and where he came from, so he should be able to point us in the direction of who bewitched him and lured him to town."

I looked up. "He will?"

"Yeah, but I'm a bit concerned I might have to take you to the hospital in his place," she said. "Why did you drink it?"

"I thought it wasn't supposed to have a strong effect on fairies," I mumbled, my face heating in shame.

"Who told you that?" she asked. "The goblins?"

"They didn't lie," I said. "Maybe there's too much human in me after all."

Not only was I supposed to be seeing my foster parents later this morning, I'd also foolishly agreed to meet up with those two fairies this afternoon as well. I couldn't cancel on them now. It was entirely my own fault I'd ended up in this state, and to add insult to injury, I'd spent hours surrounded by fairies yesterday and had utterly failed to ask them any substantial questions. Though if I had, I probably wouldn't remember anything they'd told me anyway.

"Nathan came to check on you twice last night," Alissa added. "He's worried about you."

My head throbbed. "I'll text him, but I need to get my hands on a hangover cure first. I guess I was too addled to take a hangover potion last night."

"I gathered," said Alissa. "So… did you find out anything useful at the market?"

I thought back to the last time anything had made sense. "I learned that nobody at the market sells goblin fruit, just the seeds, which take forever to grow. Does Riff remember anything about who might have lured him there?"

"Why not ask him yourself?" she asked. "My grandmother is making arrangements for him to receive some kind of memory spell that will erase his experiences, so we'll need to get all the information we can from him before then. I wanted to wait for you to wake up before I asked him anything."

"Seriously?" I said. "Are you certain he won't remember anything?"

"He has people in the normal world who might be worried about him," she replied. "If you can verify that he speaks the truth, though, I can ask Samuel to read it from your mind if it ever comes up in court."

I blinked. "Since when? I thought the vampires were against using their abilities to influence the outcome of trials."

"Vincent made an exception for you, remember?" she said. "Samuel would do the same."

"I thought it was a one-off." The idea of opening my mind to the vampires when I had so many secrets swimming in there wasn't appealing. What if the hunters found out what I knew? The more people who read my thoughts, the more likely it was that they'd realise I'd figured out their secret.

"He told me to let you know, anyway," she said. "Are you okay to come to the hospital? We can grab a coffee to go on the way. With an added hangover cure."

Somehow, I managed to dress myself despite my

banging headache, while Alissa left some food out for the cats. As Alissa had promised, we stopped by Charms & Caffeine for a mug of coffee laced with a potent hangover cure. Layla took one look at my face and gave me a large drink for the price of a small one despite my feeble protests.

"I am never taking so much as a sniff of goblin brew again," I said to Alissa on the way out, holding my coffee close to my chest like a precious object.

"I don't blame you," she said. "You'd think there'd be restrictions on the stuff, but if there were, they'd have to ban the werewolves' cocktails, too. I guess it's designed for goblins only. Even elves seem to struggle with the side effects, based on what I've seen from Thistle."

"Is he still at the hospital, then?" I took a long drink.

"Unfortunately," she answered. "I caught him trying to smuggle cocktails into his room again."

"Do you think he had a role in what happened to Riff?" I drank more coffee, relieved when the fogginess began to lift. Layla's potions worked wonders. "I admit, I'm no more enlightened than before after asking around at the market, but it strikes me as more likely to be an accident than anything. He didn't get hurt."

"He's lucky he didn't." She led the way into the hospital, and we headed through the reception area to Riff's room. Two nurses stood on either side of his bed, including Lou. He glanced at me, a slightly dazed expression on his face. At least he was no longer screaming and calling me a monster.

Lou stepped to my side and whispered, "We gave him a potion to relax him, so it doesn't hit him quite as hard when he has to forget."

"Hello," he said, looking up at Alissa and me blearily. "Wild night, wasn't it? I musta hit my head pretty hard."

"Yes, you did," said Alissa. "You're almost ready to go, but before you do, we wanted to ask a couple of questions. Do you remember drinking anything at a market?"

"Market?" he echoed. "Yeah… I guess I remember something like that. It's blurry."

"And do you remember anyone taking you there?" I put in. "Did you meet anyone before you went there, or did you walk there by yourself?"

A thoughtful look came over him. "I remember being in a field. I think my mates ditched me there, so I went walking on my own…" He trailed off.

"Yes?" said Alissa.

"Next thing I remember is waking up by a lake." He shrugged. "I went walking for a while. Everything else is a blur."

That was probably the best we'd get from him. It couldn't be clearer that he had no memory of how he'd come to be intoxicated, let alone how he'd ended up in town. If the person responsible had intended it to look like a complete accident, they'd succeeded.

I backed out into the waiting room as my phone buzzed with a message from Nathan asking if I was okay. I texted him back asking him to meet me at the hospital, and then I finished my coffee.

Lou emerged from the ward a moment later. "What in the world happened to you, Blair? You look like you've caught a bad case of flu."

"Goblin brew." I shuddered, tossing my empty coffee cup into a bin. "I should be okay when the effects of this hangover cure kick in."

"You're not the only one," she said. "The only person in a worse state than you today is Argyle."

"Who…?" I looked around and spotted a witch half-asleep in the corner of the waiting room, looking as morose as I felt. Argyle Winthrop. The name rang a bell. Wasn't she the gardener witch who Pix had mentioned? I'd been looking for her at the market yesterday, before I'd got side-tracked.

"Poor thing," said Lou. "I'd go back home to sleep it off if I were you, Blair."

Not really an option. While Lou went back into the ward, I made my way over to Argyle's corner of the waiting room.

"Hey," I said to her. "What're you here for?"

"I had a rather wild night." She hiccoughed. "I fell on a Stinging Sneezer when I got back to my shop, and it stung me."

That's when I saw that one of her hands had turned bright purple and was covered in vivid-looking boils. "So were you at the market?"

She gave another cough. "Where else would I have got this drunk?"

"Um, have you ever seen that man before?" I asked. "The one I was just visiting? He's a normal, but we think he might have found his way into the market somehow. I wondered if you saw how he got there."

"To be quite frank, I can't remember how *I* got there." She slumped in her seat. "Perhaps I was always there."

Oh, boy. I'd have to wait until she sobered up before I got any sense out of her.

"Mrs Winthrop?" asked Lou. "Come in here, now. Let's have a look at that hand of yours."

Argyle rose to her feet and tottered away. So much for that idea. Still, the odds of her maliciously targeting an ordinary person seemed low. She was in a world of her own.

As for Riff himself, he didn't seem to recall anything of the market at all. So did that mean he hadn't been there when he'd been enchanted?

Before I could figure out my next move, Madame Grey entered the hospital through the front door. "Are you all right, Blair?"

"Yeah, I'm just waiting for Nathan," I said. "We're heading…"

"To meet your foster parents," she said. "Alissa told me. I hope it's okay if I send someone to keep an eye on things from a distance. Not that I think you'll make trouble, but things have a tendency to go in unexpected directions wherever you go."

That was a kind way of saying I attracted chaos wherever I went. In truth, I should probably be more concerned about potential ways I might accidentally give away my secrets to my foster parents, but I hadn't entirely shaken off my headache yet. "You aren't wrong. Oh, Nathan's here." I spotted Nathan outside the hospital and ducked out of the doors to join him.

He greeted me with a hug. "I'm glad you're feeling better, Blair. I have to admit when you said you were at the hospital, I worried."

"Nah, I just drank a strong coffee laced with a hangover cure," I said. "There's nothing wrong with me now but a heavy dose of shame."

"So you came here to see the normal," he said. "I heard he's going home today."

"Yeah, he is, but he still doesn't remember how he ended up in that state," I explained. "He didn't remember much of the market, not that that proves anything. *I* don't remember much of yesterday, to be honest."

"Did you have the chance to talk to the goblins, then?" he asked.

"Yeah, but they gave me some of their brew and the rest is history." I grimaced. "The plus side is that I have a meeting with some fairies this afternoon, so I have a second chance to talk to them. No goblin brew will be involved, don't worry."

His forehead creased. "Are you sure?"

"Nope, but I'm not sure about introducing my foster parents to this madness, either." I took in a breath. "So… are you ready to meet them?"

———

Because no buses or trains stopped near Fairy Falls, our quickest option was to walk. Or fly. I got my wings out for a bit, not as accustomed to trekking for hours over the hills like Nathan was. I turned back to human form when we drew closer to civilisation—the town of Sloan, which, in my cover story, I called home.

Now all I had to do was divert my parents' attention from asking any questions which might poke holes in my story. No pressure.

It'd been so long since I'd been in the normal world that I'd forgotten how… banal it looked compared to Fairy Falls, with grey streets crowded with traffic and tall buildings masking the scenery. Or maybe it was just my nerves talking. Back in my old life, I'd lived in a shared house with a bunch of students who threw loud parties under my feet, bouncing between jobs as a series of disasters shunted me around in their wake. I couldn't even ride public transport without it breaking down, while computers crashed when I looked at them. Now I knew those effects were due to the barriers I'd had on my magic before moving to Fairy Falls had unlocked my real powers.

"I can't believe I went along with it," I remarked to Nathan as we walked through the ordinary high street packed with new year's shoppers. "I mean, I got offered a job I'd never applied to, was sure I'd hallucinated that the person who was talking to me on the phone was a werewolf, and still showed up for the job interview."

"I'm glad you did." He squeezed my hand. "So, you live here. Or your alter ego does, anyway."

"That's the cover story," I said. "It's not like we'd be able to hide any signs of magic if we met up in Fairy Falls. Well. The street where you live looks normal enough, but still."

Not that I hadn't done a spectacular job of wrecking our first family dinner together, regardless. No matter what else might go wrong today, I was fairly sure Nathan wouldn't sabotage things by accidentally inviting a group of elves to join us. Not to mention the pixie.

We waited outside the shopping centre in the cold, until I saw a familiar pair approaching us: an older couple, grey-haired, and utterly normal. Mr and Mrs Wilkes were both much more tanned than the last time I'd seen them, but otherwise, they looked exactly the same. Their delighted smiles tugged at something inside me, and I ran to meet them, not caring if I was behaving like a little kid.

I felt like one, too, as they swept me into a hug between them.

Then, when they released me, they turned to face Nathan.

"So this is the young man who's monopolising Blair's attention," said Mr Wilkes.

I flushed. "Dad."

"I'm Nathan." He shook my foster dad's hand. "It's great to meet you. You too, Mrs Wilkes."

She beamed at him, and I dared to relax a little. Of course they'd like Nathan. He was the postcard example of someone who didn't screw up or attract trouble at every corner like I did. Luckily for all of us, they were used to my penchant for disaster—if not the magical type. They'd raised me, after all.

We went into the cafe, where I ordered a regular coffee instead of the magical kind I normally went for, silently thanking Layla's hangover cure for holding up. Mr Wilkes insisted on sitting beside Nathan and wasted no time in engaging him in conversation.

"And what do you do?" he asked Nathan.

"I'm a security guard," he said easily. He did a pretty good job of making his job sound dull to outsiders, if you discounted the overactive werewolves, bickering shifter clans, and the hunters' constant attempts to get into our town, that is. I appreciated his effort, which was a lot better than my own clumsy attempts to skirt around an explanation of how I'd come to be hired by a recruitment company which I'd never given my CV to.

I had a few work-related anecdotes memorised just in case—stripped of any magical context—but I most definitely would not be mentioning that I'd spent most of yesterday hanging around a market full of goblins and elves while my boss skipped around under a giant umbrella with fairy wings on it. My foster parents knew I was a Harry Potter fan, but that would definitely be taking it too far.

Still, I was happy enough to let them take over the conversation with tales of their adventures in Australia, while I said as little as possible to avoid accidentally letting anything magical slip out. Just when I'd dared to begin to relax, a familiar *miaow* drew my attention. Sky sat outside the cafe, licking a paw.

"Sky!" I rose to my feet, not surprised in the least to see him lurking outside the door. At least he hadn't brought his new friends from the market along with him. "Mum, Dad, meet Sky. He's my... my new pet. I'd say I adopted him, but it's more the other way around."

A few people stared at us when I crouched down to pet him, but Sky was firmly in his normal-cat mode and didn't draw any unwelcome comments. Though that might change if the staff realised there was a cat on the doorstep. He purred, enjoying the attention as my foster parents cooed over him.

"He knows he's not allowed to come in, but he couldn't resist coming to see me." I scooped him up into my arms. "Sky does whatever he wants. He refused to let you leave without introducing himself."

"Hello, Sky," said Mrs Wilkes. "I'm Blair's mother."

A pang struck my heart. Recent developments notwithstanding, she and Mr Wilkes *were* my parents, and while they'd fielded a few questions from me on my birth parents throughout my life, I'd mostly left the subject alone. I didn't know how I'd explain how my curiosity had led to the earth-shattering discoveries I'd made in the last few months.

I certainly didn't know how I'd ever explain that my biological father was in jail. Innocent or not, there was no explanation which would fit into their neat view of the order of the universe. The fact that the paranormal hunters might have set him up via magical means and also brought about my biological mum's death were equally off-limits. It was safer to let them continue knowing nothing about the covens, or Blythe's family, or the hunters. Still…

The sound of screaming came from down the street. My heart sank, and I backed into the doorway to the café, hoping against hope that the source of the noise would pass us by.

"Is someone in trouble?" Mrs Wilkes approached the door, her husband behind her. *Please, please don't let it be anything magical. Please.*

A wild-eyed man staggered down the street, pointing at me. "Wings!"

Oh, no.

8

The man kept staggering towards me, while passers-by stopped to stare at him—and by extension, me. He wore a jacket stained with mud and a pair of dirty jeans, while his hair was tangled and his eyes too wide, looking at something that wasn't there. Or rather, something that *was* there. Namely, me.

"Wings!" he yelled. "Monsters, everywhere!"

"What's he babbling about?" someone said.

The stranger advanced towards me until I had nowhere to run except inside the café. The problem was, the door was blocked by curious onlookers, coming to see what all the racket was about. Sky made a rumbling growl, and I cringed, mentally pleading with him not to shift into his monster form

"Monsters!" yelled the man, jabbing a finger at me. "Wings!"

Wait, *could* he see Sky's monster form? Sky seemed to realise there wasn't anything he could do to help, because he jumped out of my arms and hid behind my legs. Even if there hadn't been an audience surrounding me, I'd never be able to get answers from the stranger. He had no idea where he was or what was going on.

"What's wrong?" asked Mrs Wilkes, coming out of the café. "Is he drunk?"

"Or mad?" put in Mr Wilkes from behind me.

The stranger's expression was glazed, his eyes wide open. *He has the true sight.* He saw my wings, and as long as there were no other paranormals around, I'd stick out like a troll among goblins. The stranger lunged forwards, his eyes crazed, but Nathan caught his arm, preventing him from touching me. "Whoa there," he said. "Calm down."

"Does he need help?" someone said.

"Do you know him?"

I have to do something. Hadn't Madame Grey said she was sending someone to keep an eye on me in case any of the usual chaos I attracted showed up? I scanned the streets, looking past the bewildered and wary humans, and spotted a familiar figure near the back.

Alissa. My shoulders sagged with relief. She'd be able to help the stranger without giving away the magical world in front of the humans. As I caught her eye, she lifted her wand, and in a flash of light, the man collapsed in Nathan's arms. More people crowded closer while Alissa made her way through the crowd with her wand concealed up her sleeve.

Then came a second flash of light, and everyone froze except for me, Alissa and Nathan. Alissa made her way to the man's side, crouching down. "This will only last a minute. I'll zap a cover story into their heads, so they think they saw Nathan carry him over to an ambulance, but I'll need your help, Blair."

"Sure." I reached for my wand. "What should I do?"

She glanced at Nathan. "Can you move those two back inside the cafe? The others will be a bit confused, but Blair won't have to explain herself to them."

"Sure." Nathan guided Mr and Mrs Wilkes back into the cafe. Trying not to look at their frozen expressions, I moved to help him out. Alissa joined us, engaging in some complex wand movements in front of the frozen onlookers. Then she walked outside, still waving her wand in swirling patterns that made me dizzy to watch.

There came another bright flash of light, and the man's body vanished—and so did Alissa. She reappeared an instant later, and with another wave of her wand, the crowd came back to life. Everyone moved at once, except for me. I remained standing, wondering what they thought they'd seen. Thankfully, though, nobody acted at all like they'd seen multiple people vanish in front of them.

Alissa leaned over to whisper, "I whisked him into the hospital in Fairy Falls. Then I threw an illusion spell over everyone, so all the witnesses will think they remember seeing him get carried away in an ambulance."

"Judging by the fact that nobody is panicking, I'd say it worked." I glanced at Nathan, who faced my slightly dazed-looking foster parents in the entryway to the café.

"Someone you know?" asked Mrs Wilkes.

"Ah, this is Alissa," I said to them. "A friend of mine. She's just on her way out now."

Alissa gave me a grateful nod and walked out the door, disappearing from sight. While we'd narrowly avoided a bigger scene than there might have been, now she had to handle another human who'd come into contact with the magical world, right after the first victim had recovered.

We took our seats in the café again, but the mood was ruined, my nerves on edge. Mr and Mrs Wilkes thought I was stressed about the strange man's shouting at me, and I didn't argue, because it was true. Just not for the reasons they thought.

As my gaze fell on the clock, I remember I'd already promised I'd meet up with those fairies at the market in less than an hour. I couldn't possibly be less enthused at the notion, but with someone else potentially under the effects of goblin fruit, it was more important than ever that I found out who was targeting normals.

Besides, after what I'd just witnessed, a spate of fairy drama would be a welcome relief.

———

Sky padded alongside me as I walked back to Fairy Falls, with Nathan on my other side. The sounds of the market's music and merriment drifted across the fields and hills, while the gleaming outline of the half-frozen lake drew closer by the minute.

"I don't understand how that guy found his way to the market," I said to Nathan. "You'd think security would have spotted him. The fields are surrounded."

"Yes, they are, but the market draws a strange crowd," he said. "That music doesn't help. Half the security team's reports from last night make no sense and they weren't even drinking goblin brew."

"Yeah, I can imagine." I wished there was such a thing as a selective earplug charm so I could put the eerie music on mute. "It even got me, in the end. I guess it's hard to blame goblin brew if the whole market causes people to lose their senses."

I'd drank the goblin brew knowing what I was getting into, but the market itself carried a dreamlike sensation which was always one step from transforming into a nightmare.

"I'd still put at least some of the blame on the goblins," Nathan said. "And nobody reported seeing a normal come into the market yesterday at all."

"Guess we were tempting fate by going out this morning, though," I murmured. "As soon as we turned our backs, someone else fell victim to the goblin brew."

"He might not have been to the market," he said. "Or to Fairy Falls, either. It wouldn't be difficult for someone to buy goblin brew and take it outside the market to give to unsuspecting humans. Someone who thought it was a laugh, maybe."

Hmm. Like the elf who made a habit of drunkenly wandering into normal towns, for instance. I needed to speak to him again, but first, it was almost time for me to meet up with those two fairies from yesterday. They probably remembered last night much more clearly than I did.

"I have to go and meet those two fairies now," I said to Nathan. "But I'll see you later, okay?"

"Sure." He looked down at Sky. "Will you take him with you? I don't like the idea of you potentially running into trouble again."

"I know better than to drink the goblin brew this time around." I pressed a firm kiss to his lips and wrapped my arms around him. "Have I ever said you worry too much?"

"You were almost attacked by a madman earlier."

A madman bewitched by a fairy. I heard the unspoken words. Granted, the two fairies hadn't exactly been nice to me the first time we'd met, and it'd surprised me that they'd agreed to a meeting so readily. Perhaps they planned to mug me and tie me up in a tree. Who knew how fairies' minds worked?

"Sky will out-monster the monsters, trust me," I reassured him.

"I'm going to join up with the security team over the hill," he said. "I'll be a minute's walk away if you need me."

"Sure." I released him, my nerves skittering again, and made my way downhill with Sky at my side.

As the market's clamour drew nearer, my heartbeat kicked into gear. I wouldn't have minded having Nathan to keep me company, but I needed to present myself to them as a fairy and not a witch if I wanted to get any answers. *Calm down, Blair. They won't hurt you in broad daylight.* As long as I didn't go near any goblin brew, I was safe.

I snapped my fingers and turned into my fairy mode before flitting downhill. I skirted the market, debating applying an earplug charm to block out the music. While it wouldn't have as strong an effect on me now that I wasn't drunk on goblin brew, just being nearby muddled my human senses. Several of the people who'd been dancing last night were still prancing away, wild-eyed, feet flying, limbs slick with sweat.

If I'd been more assertive and willing to engage in confrontation, I'd have gone to give those goblins a stern talking-to about their claims that goblin brew had a less strong effect on fairies, but I had zero desire to end up being turned into a toadstool. Besides, it was past three o'clock. So where were…?

There they are. The two fairies waited on the hillside, their hair loose and flowing, their wings beating behind their shoulder blades. They wore dresses patterned with flowers, and crowns of flowers woven together atop their heads. The blond one wore a red dress and the brunette wore blue, while their pointed ears and elegant features made them look like sisters.

"Hey." I flew to a halt in front of them. "I came, like I said."

"So you did." The blond fairy, Holly, giggled. "You looked like you were having a good time last night."

I smiled weakly. "Yeah, I don't think I'll be drinking any goblin brew again."

"But you did enjoy it," said her brunette companion.

"Until I woke up." I decided to push on while I had the chance. "Did you know two humans—normals, not witches or wizards or anything—have fallen under the effects of goblin brew? Both of them in the last week."

"I wouldn't know a normal from a witch," said Holly. "They look the same."

"Witches have better dress sense," added Heather. "You're not all fairy, are you? If you were, you wouldn't live here. With the humans."

I assumed that wasn't intended as an insult, but it was a little difficult to tell. Her tone was halfway between awe and disbelief.

"My mother was a witch," I explained. "She died when I was a kid. And my dad… he's a fairy."

"Your dad?" she echoed. "Who is he?"

"He's…" Wait. I didn't even know his name. He'd

always signed his letters as 'your father'. "Um. He knew Tanith Wildflower. She was my birth mother."

"Who?" asked Heather.

Argh. Why didn't I think to ask him? Of course he couldn't actually sign his correspondence, in case someone intercepted his letters, but I couldn't believe it hadn't occurred to me until now. I wished I'd asked my mum's ghost while I'd had the chance.

"Tanith was a witch," I said to them. "She lived in Fairy Falls… a few years ago."

More like decades. She and my dad had met in secret and she'd then left the town, which meant that even most people from Fairy Falls had never known my dad existed. And, of course, the fairies who hadn't lived in Fairy Falls would never have heard of Tanith.

"And she's the reason you're looking for a Pixie-Glass?" asked the blond fairy.

"Um. Yes, it is. But your friend, he said it might have—"

"MIAOW," said Sky loudly, drowning out my words.

The two fairies jumped at the sight of Sky, who exuded a surprising level of menace for such a small animal. His fur bristled, as though he was prepared to glamour himself into a giant. I shot him a pleading look, but he ignored me.

"Oh, is he a fairy cat?" Heather asked.

Sky growled. Uh-oh. "Sky can be a little… untrusting of strangers."

"Yes, they're a rare sight even in the market," said Holly, apparently unconcerned about the danger. "They generally keep to themselves. Is he a friend of yours?"

Sky continued to emit a low, threatening growl which sounded more like a tiger than a cat. "Sky, stop that."

"Miaow." Sky advanced on the two fairies, shrugging me off, and transformed into his giant monstrous cat form. A huge shaggy beast with dark fur suddenly filled the space where my cat had been sitting, and Holly and Heather jerked away from him with alarmed beats of their wings.

"What's he doing?" asked Holly.

"I have no idea," I said. "Sky, behave."

I placed a hand on his back, disarmed by how solid and giant he felt. Even knowing the monstrous disguise was a glamour, it was difficult to resist backing away from his growling and hiding from sight.

He shook me off and swatted at the two fairies with a paw. They flew backwards out of reach, and then in unison, they turned around and soared downhill, melding with the crowd heading into the market.

"Sky." I made to chase them, but I'd never catch up with two fairies fleeing at a high speed. "What was that for?"

"Miaow," he said, his voice still an unnervingly deep growl.

"Blair?" Nathan hurried over to me, eyeing Sky's monstrous form. "What did they do?"

"Nothing," I said. "Sky just chased them off when I was in the middle of asking if they knew my dad."

"Miaow." In a blink, Sky was back to his usual self, as though nothing had happened at all. He sat there and licked a paw, casual as ever.

"Did they know anything?" he asked.

I shook my head. "I don't know his name. How mad is

it that I never asked? I mean, that's the least of everything he didn't tell me, considering he was afraid the hunters might intercept his letters to me, but still. And they didn't know my mum, of course, because she wasn't a fairy. I really screwed up."

"You didn't screw up, Blair," he said. "I don't blame you for wanting to speak to them, but—"

"But the odds were against me. I know."

There were so many other questions I'd wanted to ask. Maybe my dad was unknown even among the fairies, but the leader of the hunters might not be. On the other hand, I wouldn't have done myself any favours if I'd asked how a fairy had come to rule over the most powerful anti-paranormal force in the region. Caution outweighed curiosity —for now.

My gaze travelled over the market, past the laughing, dancing crowd. Even after my night of dancing, I felt a world apart from everyone else here, weighed down by the secrets I kept.

Nathan drew me into a hug, pressed a kiss to my forehead. "It's okay, Blair. You did your best."

I exhaled in a sigh. "I guess I should head to the hospital and see how that poor guy from earlier is getting along."

———

After I'd seen Sky off—or rather, he saw himself off, striding off towards home without so much as a *miaow* of goodbye—Alissa met me outside the hospital.

"My grandmother just read me the riot act," she said. "Apparently I wasn't supposed to use the transportation spell in front of a crowd. I said I erased their memories and made sure they won't remember a thing, but she's not happy."

"It didn't look like you had much of a choice in the matter," I said. "Has anyone figured out who our new guest is, or how he ended up in that state?"

"Some other witches and wizards went undercover to the street where he showed up to see if they could find any witnesses," she said. "We have to work within our own laws, and when someone creates a scene like that, it's hard to avoid side effects."

"Namely, freaking out my foster parents," I said.

"Were they okay?" asked Alissa.

"Yeah, for a wonder," I said. "Aside from my cat inviting himself along, today actually went pretty well. My meeting with the fairies, on the other hand, was a total disaster."

She arched a brow. "You met with the fairies?"

"I wanted to ask them a few questions, but Sky Hulked out and scared them off," I said. "Now they're probably warning everyone else at the market about the fairy-witch with the mad cat."

"Maybe he thought he was protecting you," said Alissa.

"They weren't threatening me." I shook my head. "They didn't think they saw any normals at the market, either, but as they reminded me, nobody can tell the difference between a normal and a paranormal, if they both look human. Unless they have my ability, I guess, but what am I supposed to do, stand with the security team and spy on everyone who comes into the market?"

"You might not have to," she said. "That street where the guy showed up? It was right down the road from where Thistle was drunkenly wandering around the other day."

"Seriously?" I stared at her. "Have you asked him?"

"I would have, but there's a slight problem," she said. "He went missing this morning."

9

"The elf is missing?" I said to Alissa.

Seriously? Where in the world had he disappeared to this time?

"It took me a while to find out, because I wasn't on my shift when he escaped," she said. "He wasn't supposed to be discharged yet either. I assume he didn't go far, but considering the timing…"

"What—you think he went straight to Sloan and got that guy drunk on goblin brew?" I said dubiously. "And then disappeared?"

She shook her head. "I don't know. So far, we haven't been able to dredge up any witness accounts from people who saw him, but he's been unaccounted for all day."

Oh, no. Had he found his way to Sloan? It wouldn't be the first time, after all. "He didn't leave at the same time as Riff did?"

"Nope," she said. "He's supposed to have been in his ward, but the others were too busy dealing with other patients to realise he was gone until long after they'd taken

Riff away. He can't be supervised all the time, especially with people coming in and out needing care. There's only so many of us staff on duty, and a lot of people booked the weekend off to go to the market. Having said that, I don't know how he can have walked all that way without help."

Hmm. He was the one link between the normals and the market, albeit a tenuous one. Still, his disappearance couldn't be a coincidence.

"Maybe he went to see that witch who makes cocktails," I said. "He's always going on about her."

"Who is she?" Alissa asked.

"She works at the Laughing Pixie," I said. "Not sure if she'll be there now, but she makes the cocktails he likes. Perhaps he stopped by her place after he left the hospital."

"All right," said Alissa. "We'll head there. Our new visitor is sleeping right now, and we're still trying to figure out who he is and where he came from. He's not capable of giving us a coherent testimony at the moment. Oh, and we're calling him Spud. That was Ava's idea, not mine, but now it's the only name he answers to."

"All right." I turned away from the hospital and Alissa and I made our way to the Laughing Pixie. My headache was on its way back, and the smell of booze soaking into the floor of the student pub didn't help in the slightest. You'd think selling anything containing goblin fruit in here would be illegal, but then again, the other neon cocktails looked like a health hazard, too. Not to mention the floors.

Luck was with me for once, and Pix herself was working behind the bar. Her pink hair was tipped with purple today.

"Hey, Blair." She looked at Alissa, her brow wrinkled. "You're from the hospital, right? I remember seeing you carrying some of my customers out of here a couple of times."

"I expect you did," said Alissa. "I'm Alissa. We're looking for a patient of mine who sneaked out of the hospital this morning, and he spent the whole time he was under our care raving about your cocktails. He's been unaccounted for all day."

"Who?" she asked. "Was he an elf, by any chance?"

"You've got it," I said. "We're worried he might do himself an injury. I mean, worse than he already did."

"I'm afraid I haven't seen him today."

True. "When did you last see him, then?"

She hesitated. "Why do you want to know?"

Alissa's eyes narrowed. "Have you been to the hospital recently?"

The witch's shoulders slumped. "All right, so I may have smuggled him a drink or two in the hospital to cheer him up."

"That's why he took so long to get sober," I said. "Now he's running around with several broken bones, which would normally be his problem and not ours, but he may be a suspect in an ongoing investigation as well."

"Investigation?" Her brows shot up. "What kind?"

"Two humans have been found under the effects of goblin brew," I explained. "The second showed up in a normal town today and caused a scene. Given that it was the same town where Thistle himself almost exposed our world to the normals the other day, he's wanted for questioning."

"Whoa." Her eyes rounded. "I didn't know he'd shown magic to any normals."

"He didn't need to use magic. Just running around in public would have been enough to freak most people out." I gave an eye-roll. "The two normals in this case, though… they were under the influence of some pretty strong hallucinations."

"You didn't give any of your drinks to other hospital patients?" asked Alissa.

"No, of course not," she said. "I only visited Thistle because he specifically asked me to. I didn't speak to anyone else."

True. She hadn't seen Riff, then. Not in the hospital, at least.

"Including any of the staff," added Alissa. "What did you do, use an invisibility potion to get in? Or a diversion spell?"

"I swear, I wasn't involved in his disappearance," she said. "I bet he shows up here sooner or later, though. He always does."

"Can you give us a call if he does?" I asked. "Tell him he's wanted at the hospital."

She nodded. "Of course I will."

Alissa and I headed for the doors. I cast one last glance around the pub in case the elf was lurking in a corner somewhere, but if Pix had been truthful, she hadn't seen him since before his escape.

Alissa let the pub door swing closed behind us. "Do you reckon she's involved?"

"She's not lying," I said. "She also doesn't sell goblin brew. If she did, this wouldn't be the first time we'd have had this kind of trouble."

"Doesn't mean she didn't buy some from the market anyway," said Alissa. "I can't believe she got in and out of the hospital without being seen. She must have used an illusion or a disguise spell. Seems an awful lot of trouble to go to for one elf."

"It sounds like he's responsible for half the pub's business, though." I thought of Argyle, the gardener witch. "Is Argyle Winthrop still in the hospital?"

"Argyle?" she echoed. "Nope. We fixed her arm and sent her home. She'll be sleeping it off and avoiding the market until she recovers, if she has any sense."

"She was drunk on goblin brew," I said. "And she was one of the first people from Fairy Falls to go to the market."

"Uh, so were you, Blair," she pointed out. "We're going to need more clues if we're to track down who's manipulating normals, and I'd say we should deal with the elf first."

With no other options at hand, we walked back to the market. For all I knew, Argyle Winthrop would be here, too. Like the elf, she didn't seem to learn from her mistakes. Then again, judging by the growing crowd dancing in front of the band on the hillside, they weren't the only ones. I didn't see the elf among the frolicking dancers, and considering he should still be wearing a cast on his broken arm, he ought to be noticeable enough.

I scanned the crowd, my gaze snagging on the goblin brew stall. The goblins both broke into raucous laughter at the sight of me, banishing all hopes I might have had that they'd forgotten what a colossal fool I'd made of myself the previous night.

"Having fun?" one of them asked.

My face turned scarlet. "No thanks to your goblin brew. Why didn't you tell me it would have such a strong effect on me?"

"It's different for everyone," he said. "Maybe you're a lightweight."

I ignored the jab. "Have you seen any elves today?"

"Those two?" He pointed at a stall staffed by two elves.

"An elf wearing a cast on his arm," I elaborated. "He's missing from the local hospital, and we think he may have wandered into the market. He has a habit of getting intoxicated."

"He's in good company." The two of them burst into laughter again.

"Yes, but he's also injured and is wanted back in the hospital," said Alissa.

"We didn't see an elf who fits that description, little witch," said one of the goblins.

True.

"Then have you seen a human?" I asked. "Another normal showed up under the effects of goblin brew. That's two this week."

"They've finally found a sense of fun?" he said.

"It's illegal," Alissa said.

"You and your uppity witch coven can put your pointy hats back on," he said. "We don't sell to normals. Look for your lost elf elsewhere."

So we did. We went from stall to stall, speaking to humans and goblins, elves and others, and yet nobody had a word to say about an elf wearing a cast.

"He didn't take the cast off, did he?" I remarked to Alissa. "Because that would explain why they didn't recognise him."

"He shouldn't have," she said. "Unless he used a potion or spell to fix his broken arm, that is. We were waiting until he sobered up to ask if he wanted us to use magic to fix it, but I didn't realise that he had someone smuggling him drinks in the hospital."

We began another circuit of the market again. As we did so, Alissa's steps went jerky, and when the band changed to a faster tune, she began to skip along with the beat.

"Not you, too." I grabbed her arm and hauled her out of the market. I should have known her wilder streak would come out in close proximity to the merriment. In contrast, all I had was a screaming headache, and I had too much pride to ask the goblins where I might buy a cure. Knowing my luck, one of the fairies would trick me into taking a tonic that turned me into a mushroom or something.

Somehow, I managed to get both of us out of the market without either of us falling into the fairies' trap.

"C'mon, we should head back into town," I told her. "That's enough revelry for me."

"But what about the elf?" Alissa protested. "He might be dancing with the others."

"If he is, then I expect he'll be checking into the hospital again by tomorrow," I said. "With another injury."

Her expression cleared as the sounds of merriment drifted away. "I'd like to believe you're wrong, but knowing his track record, you're probably right. Let's go home."

We walked away from the market, towards the large expanse of the lake. Normally, merpeople and nereids swam in the shallows, but now the lake was partially frozen, its rippling surface undisturbed by movement. I'd heard the merpeople migrated to warmer places in the winter months, and I understood why. The freezing air bit at my exposed hands, while my headache continued to pound behind my eyes.

As I looked downhill, I spotted a small figure wandering around near the lake. I pointed him out to Alissa, and her lips pressed together. "Elves. I hope they're not up to mischief."

As we drew closer to the lake, another elf appeared in the shallows of the water to join his friend. They both walked along the path to the forest, singing to themselves. Neither of them was someone I recognised, but given the state of them, there was a high chance of them wandering onto the shifters' territory by accident.

"Where are they going?" Alissa whispered.

"I can't tell if they're from the elf king's people or not." I walked closer to the singing elves and called out, "Excuse me?"

"Hello, fair one," said one of the elves, nearly tripping over his own feet in the shallows. "Have you come to show us to the falls?"

"Are you one of the elf king's people?" I asked. "Because if not, I don't think he'll take kindly to you wandering in his woods. Neither will the werewolves."

They wouldn't want *me* showing up without warning when I hadn't figured out who'd bewitched those two humans yet, either. Especially when they believed the goblins were responsible and didn't seem inclined to take responsibility for Thistle's wild antics.

"And do the falls belong to anyone?" the elf enquired.

"The falls?" I echoed. "No, but if you want to go there, you might want to sober up first."

The route to the waterfall was treacherous enough even when you weren't inebriated, as I'd discovered when I'd had to use my levitating boots or wings to get down the hill without face-planting into the lake. *Please say that's not what Thistle did.*

"Where did you come from?" Alissa interjected.

"That way." The two elves both pointed in different directions, then burst into hysterical laughter.

Just what we needed. Two intoxicated elves who *weren't* the one we were looking for.

The sound of someone clearing their throat came from the bushes, and two more elves stepped out on the path. One of them was Bramble, and the other was his friend Twig. I opened my mouth to ask if they knew the pair of newcomers, but a sudden flash of light ignited in Bramble's hands.

Whoa. I backed up as the air went static with lightning, and the two elves fled along the lakeside, back towards the market.

Bramble and Twig regarded their flight with expressions of satisfaction on their faces.

"Was that really necessary?" I said. "I doubt they were coming here to threaten you or your king. They just got lost."

"Market elves are nothing but trouble," growled Bramble.

"Thought it was the goblins you didn't like." I folded my arms. "Speaking of trouble, have you seen Thistle? He sneaked out of the hospital and went missing somewhere."

"That shameful excuse for an elf has not been seen in the forest," Twig said. "Why do you want to speak to him?"

"Another human fell victim to the effects of goblin brew," I explained. "One who wasn't anywhere near Fairy Falls."

"You said you would find the culprit," said Twig. "You mean to say another human fell under the spell while you were watching?"

"It didn't happen when I was watching," I protested. "I was out visiting my foster parents in Sloan and had no idea until he showed up."

"I hear you spent last night partying with the goblins instead," Bramble growled. "Drinking their brew and acting the fool."

Great. Even the local elves had heard the story. "I was trying to find out if anyone at the market had seen any normals, that's all. I didn't mean to get drunk."

"The goblins are not trustworthy," said Bramble. "They came here for nothing but mischief."

"I don't disagree, but Thistle is just as bad," I replied. "Can you let me know if you see him? I promise I'll try to find out who bewitched those normals."

"Do not delay any longer, Blair Wilkes." Bramble disappeared into the bushes without another word. His companion followed an instant later.

Only then did I remember that I'd intended to talk to them about my dad—not that there was much chance that the elf king would share another helpful word with me if he'd heard the story of my misadventures at the market last night.

"Are they always that abrupt?" Alissa scanned the

bushes for any more wandering elves. "We'd better go before they come back and chase us off."

"Nah, they won't," I said. "It's the market folk they don't like, and I've just proved their point. I don't know why I believed a word those goblins said."

All the same, I remained convinced that someone outside the market had bewitched those two normals, with or without goblin brew. As far as my lie-sensing power could work out, none of the people I'd questioned had set eyes on a normal inside the market.

Alissa checked her phone. "Sounds like our new arrival is awake. Want to see if we can get any sense out of him?"

"All right," I said. "It's worth a shot."

We walked away from the lake, towards the high street and into the town once more. There weren't as many people wandering around the streets as there normally would have been, and even Charms & Caffeine looked unusually empty despite its invitingly warm atmosphere. Everyone seemed to be at the market instead.

Since my headache was back, I went to get another hangover cure on the way to the hospital.

"Hey, Blair," said Layla. "Same again?"

"Make it a double, and you can keep the change." Layla's business was probably suffering due to the market being here, so it was the least I could do.

As I turned away from the counter, my gaze fell on the only customer inside the cafe. Thistle the elf sat at a table under the window, nursing a mug of coffee. *You've got to be kidding me.*

10

"He was here all along?" I whispered to Alissa.

Alissa walked over to the elf's table. "There you are," she said. "Where have you been all day?"

Thistle hiccoughed. "I have seen many things and been to many places."

"Like Sloan?" I asked. "The human town? Another normal human showed up intoxicated in front of normal witnesses, and it happened shortly after you disappeared this morning."

"How unfortunate," said the elf, nearly knocking over his drink with his elbow.

"We sent out a search party for you," Alissa said, exasperated. "The entire hospital was involved. You can't just walk out of there without being discharged. Everyone thought you'd gone back to the market."

"The market?" he said. "It's far too noisy. My head is in a delicate condition."

"That's your own fault," said Alissa. "We found out

about Pix, too. You can't have someone sneaking you cocktails in the hospital. It's against the rules."

"Don't speak so loudly." He raised his hands over his head and let out a faint moan.

Alissa rolled her eyes. "Personally, I think you should have been discharged today anyway, but that doesn't change the fact that you're wanted for questioning."

He hiccoughed. "By whom?"

"By us." I pulled out a chair and took a seat opposite him. "A normal showed up under the influence of goblin brew not far from the spot where you yourself caused a scene in front of normals the other day."

"You accuse me of such a thing?" He rose to his feet and tried to flee, but tripped over a chair leg and landed in a heap at Alissa's feet.

"Everything all right?" Layla called from behind the counter.

"How long has this elf been in here?" I asked her.

"Since midday," she said.

That meant he'd been sitting here when my foster parents and I had been at the cafe… but that didn't mean he hadn't had time to get up to mischief before then. We didn't know whereabouts the second victim had been before he'd shown up in Sloan, after all.

"Just tell us if you left Fairy Falls today, and we'll leave you in peace," Alissa told the elf. "Did you see any normals or didn't you?"

"I have not left this wondrous town, not I." He stumbled to his feet, catching his balance against the table. "But I may do so now, if you do not leave me be."

"He's not lying," I muttered to Alissa. "Where's his cast?"

"Did you take a potion to heal your injuries?" she asked him.

"He asked for a shot of healing potion in his coffee," Layla said. "I thought that was for his hangover. Didn't know you had a runaway patient."

"There's no point in him coming back to the hospital now," Alissa said. "Thistle, are you absolutely certain you haven't seen a normal today?"

"Not to my knowledge." He tripped away from the table, tottering towards the door. "But alas, I cannot tell my ear from my elbow."

And he was gone, the door swinging behind him.

"Did he at least pay for his drink?" asked Alissa.

"He did," said Layla. "What was all that about?"

"He sneaked out of the hospital before getting discharged," Alissa explained. "We've been running around looking for him all day, assuming he was at the market."

"Oh." Her brow wrinkled. "He's been here most of the day. I don't think he's got himself injured again."

"Good," said Alissa. "Or not," she added to me, on the way out. "At least if he's in the hospital, we can keep an eye on him."

"Except when it comes to sneaky cocktail deliveries and early morning escapades," I said.

"Seriously," she said. "To think we spent all that time searching the market. Thanks for not letting me get caught in the fairies' spell, Blair."

"What are friends for?" I sipped my coffee, feeling my headache subside a little. "Should we go to the hospital? If our new visitor is awake, we might as well see if he remembers anything about how he came to end up on that street."

Outside, it was already getting dark, the winter sun sinking over the rooftops, and the other elves' words hung over me like a personification of my hangover. It wasn't like I hadn't tried to find the culprit, despite what the elf king and his two friends seemed to think. Maybe I'd have better luck speaking to the second victim and seeing if he remembered any details of his arrival in Sloan.

"It's quiet in here," I remarked, as we entered the hospital. "Granted, the way things are going at the market, it'll be packed by morning."

Alissa pulled a face. "I wish they'd have more sense, but I nearly ended up falling into the fairies' trap myself."

"I understand why the elves suspect the goblins of being up to no good," I acknowledged. "I just don't see how they'd have had time to wander an hour away to bewitch a human before going back to set up their stall at the market. The guy had to have ended up in Sloan by walking on foot. It's not like he flew there or anything."

"Yeah, I still have people looking around Sloan trying to figure out how he came to be there," said Alissa. "But without a coherent story from the guy himself, it's just guesswork."

With any luck, he might at least be able to give enough details to point us in the direction of whoever was responsible for his predicament.

We found Spud in the same ward and the same bed which Riff had vacated. He lay there, looking quite peaceful, but he startled upright when we entered the room.

"Monsters!" he said.

"What do you remember?" Alissa asked in a calm voice. "Before the monsters?"

He shook his head frantically, then pointed at me. "Wings."

"I'm not going to harm you." Poor guy. Seeing through my glamour without expecting it had to have hit him pretty hard. Didn't stop me from feeling like a circus freak all the same, though. "And you're safe here. But we'd really like to know how you came to lose your memory. Did you drink something?"

"I don't know," he mumbled. "Maybe."

"Do you remember who gave it to you?" Alissa pressed.

"Did you see any elves?" I asked. "Not... uh, not like the ones in *Lord of the Rings*. Little elves. More like Gollum, only not quite as ugly."

It was a good job Thistle wasn't around at the moment. I doubt he'd be impressed at my description.

"Elves!" he said. "Tall, yes, very tall."

"What?" said Alissa. "No, elves aren't tall. Did you see anyone small with pointed ears?"

"Or wings?" *Fairies* fitted that description. But I'd have seen if any other fairies were wandering around the streets of Sloan while I'd been there. Right?

He began to rock back and forth, his eyes wide. "Monsters with wings, wings with monsters."

Did a fairy cause him to end up in that state? Surely not the two fairies who'd met with me, but there'd been a lot of others at the market, and I hadn't exactly been at my most observant.

We couldn't get another word of sense out of Spud, no

matter how many questions we tried. Eventually, we opted to leave him in peace.

"How long will it take to wear off?" I whispered to Alissa as she closed the door behind us.

"I'd say a day or two, but it depends how much he drank," she said. "The last guy took more than a day to start making sense."

"Guess I got lucky." My hangover wasn't entirely gone, but the aftereffects of goblin brew would be one hell of an alarming introduction to the magical world.

"Yeah, normals get the worst of it," she said. "The shock of seeing through glamour doesn't help."

"No kidding," I said. "I didn't know I looked that monstrous to people."

I was joking, kind of, but my failed meeting with the fairies had brought all my worries screaming back. What if one of them *had* been involved? Maybe the elves had good reason to be paranoid, after all.

As for Spud's current state? I couldn't help wondering if the goblin fruit theory had merit. Sure, I'd woken up feeling like I'd been kicked in the head by a group of elves, but I'd at least remembered my name. But if the market didn't sell goblin fruit, where else might the victims have found it?

Alissa snorted. "Blair, he thought *I* was monstrous, too. I mean, I did spring an unexpected transportation spell on him and drag him from one town to another with no warning. It's bound to leave a couple of side effects. I'd give it a day or two until he's back to normal and we can take him back where we found him. No harm done."

"I hope you're right." The market wouldn't be in town

for much longer, which increased the odds of the person responsible finding another victim before it moved on to its new destination. If they were from Fairy Falls, that is. But what might they have to gain from tormenting normals?

"Personally, I think Riff got hit worse because that bloody elf smuggled his cocktails into the hospital and shared them around," said Alissa. "Next time he's in here, he'll be under constant watch."

"But we're reasonably confident this dude hasn't had contact with Thistle," I added. "Unless he learned to teleport from Charms & Caffeine."

But now he was free to roam the town, including the market, unless we found more evidence to prove he'd been involved with the normals' plight. Since none of Spud's words seemed to point at an elf being responsible, we had to leave him be, for now.

In the end, I was too tired from the day's events to do any more poking around, so I went home with Alissa. Inside the flat, I found Sky sprawled on the sofa, snoring gently. He didn't wake up when we entered, but the instant I put some food out for the cats, he appeared at my side. "Miaow."

"Miaow yourself," I said. "Going to tell me why those two fairies offended you so much?"

"Miaow." He butted past me and stuck his head in the food bowl. All right, then.

After washing my hands, I joined Alissa on the sofa. "I don't know why he flipped out when I went to meet those fairies. They weren't doing anything untrustworthy."

"Usually, he's looking out for you, isn't he?" said Alissa.

"Yeah, but it'd be nice to understand what he's thinking sometimes." I glanced at Sky, who was currently swatting Roald away from his own food bowl. "He's prone to chasing off people he doesn't like, but maybe he was worried I was going to run away and join the fairies."

Not happening. I didn't belong among them, and while I longed to know more about my dad, they hadn't known who he was. Why would they? He'd been arrested years ago.

"Miaow," said a voice from behind my head. I twisted in my seat and spotted another little black cat sitting there in the doorway.

"Friend of yours?" I asked Sky.

"Is that—" Alissa rose to her feet. "Is that another fairy cat?"

"I saw him hanging out with a few of them at the market yesterday," I told her. "Not sure if they have owners…"

"Miaow," said Sky.

Alissa snorted. "I think he just said he owns *you*, not the other way around."

He probably wasn't wrong. I hesitantly approached the other fairy cat. Like Sky, he was small and black with one white paw, except for him, it was one of his back paws rather than his front ones. He had one silvery grey eye, one blue one.

"Miaow," said the newcomer.

"What is it?" I said. "Want some food? If Sky's willing to share, you're welcome to it."

I was pretty sure the cats at the market were either strays or tagged along wherever the market travelled to, but he seemed to understand me. The cat obligingly padded across the room to join Sky at the food bowl.

Roald gave him a distrustful look and slunk away behind the sofa.

"Miaow," said another voice.

"Oh, no," said Alissa.

I turned to look where she pointed. Yet another little cat sat underneath the window. "How'd you get in?"

"Miaow," said Sky.

"I think when you let one of them in, they all assumed they were invited inside," Alissa said. "Do we have enough food for all of them?"

"All of…" I trailed off. No fewer than *five* cats sat in the kitchen, as though they'd walked through the walls… which, being fairy cats, they probably had.

This is going to be an interesting night.

We dug out the spare food bowls and left out some sustenance for our visitors, but the instant I turned my back, two of the fairy cats got into a tussle over the bowl. One turned to the size of a lion, swiping at the other, who transformed into a giant beast to match him. The two shaggy monsters squared up to one another, growling.

"Hey, cut that out!" I said, alarmed. "No turning into monsters in the house, that clear?"

"MIAOW," said Sky.

To my surprise, the two cats turned normal-sized again, looking chastened.

"Sky's asserting his dominance," said Alissa. "I can't even believe this. Has anyone ever seen so many fairy cats in the same place before?"

"We've probably set some kind of record," I remarked.

Two more fairy cats appeared on the sofa, both tabbies. By now, there were at least a dozen new cats and not enough food to go around.

"Can you teach me how to do that?" I asked Sky. "Walk through walls, I mean?"

"Miaow." Sky shook his whiskers at me.

"Does that mean no? What about turning into a monster, then?" I asked.

"Miaow." Translation: just use glamour. Okay, then.

I snapped my fingers and turned invisible. Then I turned visible again. Nope, that wasn't it. I'd learned to glamour myself invisible through practising for hours—and accidentally turning the cats invisible in the process—but had yet to learn how to do anything else with it. Except for switching back and forth between my human and fairy glamours, of course.

Even the books from the library on using fairy magic hadn't explained the mechanics of using that power, so my best bet was learning from another fairy.

"Miaow." Sky padded over to me with another shake of his whiskers. In a blink, he was monster-sized, towering over six feet tall with shaggy fur. "MIAOW."

I suppressed the urge to back away. He might look nothing like my cat, but he wouldn't hurt me.

Alissa gave me a wary look. "What's he doing?"

"Demonstrating, I think." I held up my right hand, feeling for that indescribable spark of power that I barely needed to think about before glamouring myself invisible. Then in a snap of my fingers, I vanished again. "Nope. That's not it."

"Miaow." One of the cats turned into a giant beast. Then another. Within a few seconds, the whole room was full of huge shaggy creatures.

"How do you normally turn invisible, Blair?" asked Alissa, watching the whole display with a baffled expression on her face. Roald fled into her arms and she scooped him up against her chest. "Don't worry, they won't hurt you."

"I guess I just picture it in my head." I let my gaze pan over the group of monstrous giant cats. "Right?"

"Miaow," said a dozen voices.

This was by far the weirdest magic lesson I'd ever had, and that was saying a lot. I fixed the image of the giant beast in my head and snapped my fingers, but nothing happened.

"Maybe I should start with something simpler," I relented.

"Something human-sized, maybe," said Alissa.

I cast my mind around. Then I focused on Alissa and snapped my fingers. Once again, no accompanying flash of glitter appeared. One of the cats turned back to his usual size and took advantage of the others' distraction to raid the food bowls.

"C'mon." I snapped my fingers, picturing Alissa's face in my mind's eye. "I know this is the trick to it—"

Alissa gasped aloud. I turned on the spot, and Sky *miaowed* at me. "Did it work?" My voice sounded the same, but from the look on Alissa's face, I'd done *something.*

I crossed the room and ducked into the corridor leading to the bathroom. Through the open door, Alissa's reflection stared back at me from the mirror.

It worked. I looked exactly like Alissa.

"Wow, Blair," she said, her voice hushed. "I've seen transformation spells, but... that's on another level."

I grinned, and Alissa's reflection grinned back. Okay, that was weird, but cool. If I could turn into Alissa, maybe

I could do more with my newfound talent. I returned to the living room and snapped my fingers, turning back into Blair. "Who should I do next?"

"Miaow," said Sky.

"What, you?" I fixed the image of the little cat in my head and snapped my fingers.

A rushing sensation pushed me backwards onto the floor. When I looked up, the ceiling was suddenly much higher than before, while my hands—no, *paws*—touched down on the carpet.

Whoa.

Alissa peered down at me. "Uh. Blair, are you there?"

"Miaow," I said.

"MIAOW," Sky said back, taking a swipe at my nose. Startled, I tripped backwards and turned into my human form again.

I caught my balance against the sofa. "Okay, I'm not trying to usurp your position as the one and only Sky."

"Miaow," said Sky, which probably meant, *you'd better not.*

"But I can borrow your monster form?" I asked.

Alissa snorted. "I can see you getting up to all sorts of mischief with that."

"Definitely." I focused on the image of the giant beast, then snapped my fingers again. This time, nothing happened. "I guess I need more practise."

The cats clustered around me, meowing instructions. *Definitely the weirdest magic lesson I've ever had.*

Still, I was faring better at this than I had at the defensive spells I'd learned earlier in the week. Maybe I wasn't a total failure of a fairy, after all.

11

A flash of glitter woke me from a fitful sleep. Then, a small winged creature flitted past my line of sight, drawing my eyes fully open.

I sat bolt upright in bed. "There you are!"

The pixie flitted around the bed and came to a halt in mid-air. Delicate gossamer wings sprouted from his shoulder blades, while tufts of blond hair stuck up between his pointed ears. Since Sky had scared him off the last time I'd seen him, the pixie hadn't come to call on me in weeks, let alone actually come inside my room. Given the sheer number of cats roaming around our flat last night, it was a wonder he hadn't been terrified off. The noise had finally quietened down around midnight, when the cats had presumably sneaked out to the market again. Judging by the quietness in the flat, they'd stayed out all night, too.

"What is it?" I whispered. "Do you have a message from my dad?"

I scrambled for my notebook and pen, but the pixie flew into my path, tugging at the sleeve of my pyjama top.

"Huh?" I dropped the pen. "What's wrong?"

The pixie made agitated chittering noises.

"You can't deliver messages?" I guessed. "Because—I know the truth about the Inquisitor now. I know how risky it was for you to bring those messages from my dad to me. I'm sorry I didn't realise sooner."

At the word *Inquisitor*, the pixie let out a shrill moan and tried to hide underneath the bed.

"Hey—it's okay, he's not in town," I whispered. "I just wanted to tell you I figured it out. Some of it, anyway. I know there are fairies among the hunters. Not all of them are bad, but I'm guessing the ones that *are* were responsible for tossing my dad in jail. And I need a Pixie-Glass to contact him. Do you know how I might find one?"

The pixie flew out from underneath the bed, nodding frantically.

I leaned over the edge. "What's that mean? The Pixie-Glass is gone. I heard at the market that Blythe's mother of all people was the last person to look for one, and if she succeeded, I bet she handed it right over to the hunters before she was jailed."

The pixie gave a head-shake and flew over to the window, jabbing a finger in the direction of the garden.

"What… you want to go outside?" I pushed the covers aside and slid out of bed. "All right, but give me five minutes to get dressed, and please don't disappear. I know it's risky, what you're doing, but I need your help. Badly."

I hurried to find my clothes and pull them on, my hands shaking. I didn't dare hope there might be a chance of finding the Pixie-Glass after all, but the pixie's reappearance had lifted my mood all the same. Thankfully, the pixie was still there when I came out of my room, flying in circles around the living room.

As I'd suspected, Sky had vanished during the night, along with his fellow fairy cats. Not before eating all our cat food and leaving a layer of hair on every piece of furniture and every inch of carpet, though. Alissa wasn't awake yet, so I dropped her a note and slipped out of the house, shivering in the freezing air.

Nobody seemed to be on the streets. Probably, they were all sleeping off their hangovers from dancing the night away with the fairies. I couldn't see if there was any activity going on at the market from this far off, but even the dancing fairies had to sleep at some point. The pixie, however, angled through the centre of town instead of towards the lake.

"Where are you going?" I hurried along behind him, snapping my fingers to bring out my fairy wings. "The forest? The elves don't want me to come back until I've done a favour for them—they want me to find the person who bewitched two humans and gave them the true sight. I don't suppose you've seen anyone from the market handing out goblin brew to normals, or otherwise putting spells on them?"

The pixie himself had been at the centre of trouble on at least one occasion, but he'd have nothing to gain by bewitching normals. He'd probably spent the last few weeks lying low to avoid the hunters.

Instead of answering, the pixie picked up speed, forcing me to fly faster to follow him. He veered away from the forest, into the more affluent side of town where the houses were larger and more spread out. Then he flew over the fence of an elegant house surrounded by high fences, hovering above the gate.

Blythe's old house. She didn't live there anymore, and neither did Rebecca, but the hairs rose on my arms at the memory of how their mother had threatened me in this very spot.

"You're not seriously saying we should break in?" I hissed at the pixie.

He ignored me and vanished. *Glamour.* It couldn't be more obvious the pixie wanted me to hide myself and follow him on his breaking-and-entering spree.

Does that mean the Pixie-Glass is here?

If I broke in, I'd hardly be helping my family's reputation as criminals, but Mrs Dailey was in jail, Blythe had left town, and Rebecca had a new guardian. If there was the slightest chance the Pixie-Glass was inside the house, I had to look for it. With glamour, nobody would need to know I'd been here at all.

I snapped my fingers, glamouring myself invisible. Then I flew over the fence, hovering above the stone path leading to the front door. On either side, the garden had grown wild, the neat rows of flowers I'd seen last time spilling out of their beds. Not surprising, since nobody had been around to take care of the place. Mrs Dailey had always seemed like the kind of person who'd have servants to do mundane chores for her, but perhaps she hadn't expected to ever return.

But what had she done with the Pixie-Glass?

My heartbeat drummed against my ribcage as I flew up to the door, careful to avoid the purple flowers which were known to be deadly to fairies and pixies alike. The house featured in my nightmares more than I cared to admit, but Mrs Dailey was in prison for life. She couldn't appear in the hallway and hand me over to the police—or, as she'd threatened to do once before, strip out my memories of magic altogether and cast me back into the ordinary world. *Relax, Blair. Look for the Pixie-Glass. That's what you're here for.*

I withdrew my wand and cast an unlocking spell on the door, and it sprang open, revealing polished floors now covered in a thick layer of dust. It was odd not seeing my reflection in the mirror as I flew past, but I didn't quite dare take the glamour off in case she'd left a magical security camera behind or something.

All right. I'm in. Now... where do I start looking?

The house was pristine yet held an empty, abandoned air that made sense with its owner jailed and both Dailey siblings gone. Rebecca would have taken her possessions to Mrs Farringdon's house when she moved out, while Blythe had probably wanted as few reminders of home as possible.

I headed upstairs, following the trail of glittering light left by the pixie. Rebecca's room was nearly empty aside from the furniture, as I'd expected. The room next door, however, was full of boxes of dusty toys. I looked around at the bright wallpaper with some confusion. Was this Blythe's childhood room? She hadn't lived in this house when we'd first met, but she'd been forced to move back in with her mother after she'd been fired from her job at Dritch & Co for trying to get me thrown out of town. My gaze panned over shelves of books and boxes of toys, and the image of a small girl in pigtails leapt out at me from a photograph on the windowsill. At first, I didn't recognise her as Blythe, but the girl in the photograph wore the trademark snooty expression I'd often been on the receiving end of. She might have been spoiled and had everything she wanted, but Blythe had never struck me as a particularly happy person. Not even when she'd been under the influence of her sister's personality-altering spell.

Okay, that was about enough empathising with my former mortal enemy for one day. I backed out of the room, feeling weirdly ill at ease, and made my way towards the partly open door of the master bedroom at the end of the corridor. The room, however, was as empty as Rebecca's, with the furniture stripped bare and no other signs of habitation around.

I was right. Someone cleared out the place.

"Question is, who?" I muttered. "Any ideas?"

The pixie didn't answer.

As for the Pixie-Glass? Why would Mrs Dailey even need a magical communication device, anyway? Didn't she have a phone?

The pixie chittered, and a spiral of glitter drew my eyes up to the ceiling, where a trapdoor stood out behind a chandelier. *Hello, a clue.*

I flew up and aimed an unlocking spell at the trapdoor, which sprang open, revealing torrents of dust. I coughed explosively, screwing up my eyes as I flew up into the attic. Dusty cardboard boxes lay everywhere, wreathed in spiderwebs.

Landing on the floorboards, I eased the lid open of the nearest box, closing my eyes against the spray of dust. The contents appeared to be nothing but papers. A quick check of the next box confirmed the same filled that one, too. I crawled across the floor, the dusty floorboards digging into my knees, and gasped. A photo frame lay atop one of the boxes, and the woman in the photo stood out as achingly familiar, even though I'd only seen her as a ghost. Her long curly dark hair bounced to her shoulders, while her smile was a mirror of mine.

Why in the world did Blythe have a photo of my mother in her attic?

Impulsively, I grabbed the photo and stuck it into my coat pocket. It wasn't what I'd come for, but it was literally gathering dust in here and Blythe seemed to have no intention of sorting out her mother's possessions. There wasn't much else in the attic, though—just more boxes of papers and notes. Was the Pixie-Glass even here? It didn't appear so, but the pixie had gone awfully quiet.

That's when I heard a creaking noise in the house below.

Oh, no.

I dropped out of the trapdoor and closed it behind me, my wings beating as I fluttered in mid-air. There was no way to open the window and escape without making even more noise that would alert the new arrivals, so I flew out of the master bedroom into the hallway, hoping my invisibility stayed active. Was Blythe back in town already? What were the odds?

I flew to the top of the stairs, peering down into the hallway. *Someone* was here, but all I could make out was a human-shaped blur in front of the doors. Two blurs, in fact. Two intruders, both wearing… *Glamour.*

I screwed up my eyes, concentrating hard. Then, the two fairies I'd met at the market appeared in front of the door, flickering around the edges. It was definitely them, but what in the world were they doing here? They weren't local, and they hadn't even recognised my mother's name when I'd spoken to them.

They're breaking and entering. Does that mean they're on Blythe's mother's side or against her? Whatever the case, it seemed Sky had had it right when he hadn't trusted them.

"Maybe she took it with her," whispered one of the fairies. "They said she moved out of town, right?"

"Yeah, but this is the only place she's known to have lived," said the second fairy. "If she hid it, it stands to reason that she might have locked it in a safe here or something. Somewhere it wouldn't be found while she was in jail."

I remained frozen in place, rigid with shock. *They're looking for the Pixie-Glass.*

It seemed they hadn't lied when they'd said the last one had been sold, but they must have found out Mrs Dailey had been the owner. Then they'd come here to find it. To sell, it maybe. Or to give it to the hunters, assuming they didn't already have it.

I remained absolutely still, though I was sure my fast-beating heart was audible throughout the whole house. I looked around for the pixie, but of course he'd glamoured himself invisible, too.

Why are they here? Blythe hadn't had any fairy friends. She'd hated me for being a fairy and done her best to make my life a misery for that very reason. She and I were distantly related, but while my mum had fallen in love with a fairy, Blythe's family was all human. Which meant the two intruders were no friends of hers, whoever they were.

I hovered above the stairs, wondering if I should slip outside and call the police, but the fairies moved through the hall decisively, not seeing me waiting on the stairs. I could just picture what Steve would say if I called him and said someone was breaking into Mrs Dailey's house—and how was I supposed to explain it without giving away my own wrongdoing?

I had a better idea. Time to use my best asset... the element of surprise.

I snapped my fingers to turn visible and landed in front of them. The two fairies let out startled cries.

"Quiet!" one hissed to the other. "It's just Blair. What are you doing here?"

"I could ask you two the same question." I looked between them. "You're looking for the same thing I am, aren't you?"

"I *told* you we shouldn't have got her attention." The blond fairy, Holly, groaned. "Now we're trespassing in a human's house, and if we get caught—"

"It'd be your own fault," I finished. "Why do you need the Pixie-Glass? I thought you were the ones who sold it."

"We weren't," said Heather.

The sound of the door slamming made the fairies jump—and they vanished in a blur of glamour. I snapped my fingers and did the same, my heart lurching into my boots as Steve the gargoyle elbowed his way through the front door.

"I heard voices," Steve growled. "Who's hiding?"

Two more gargoyles stood at his shoulders, totally blocking the way out. I'd have to escape through the back door. At least it wasn't the hunters, but it seemed the fairies weren't as accomplished at breaking and entering as they thought they were. And someone had drawn the police's attention. Who?

The last thing I needed was to wind up locked in one of Steve's cells, so I flew through the house and aimed for the back door. If the other two fairies got caught in here, it wasn't my problem.

With a wave of my wand, I opened the back door and found myself in the garden where I'd met Mrs Dailey for the first time. The once neat flowerbeds were overgrown, the hedges in dire need of trimming. It seemed Mrs Dailey hadn't arranged for anyone to take care of the place while she was in jail… so who had been watching the house? Someone must have been, in order for the police to show up so quickly.

I flew above the house, aiming towards the high street. When I passed a couple of witches who pointed up at me with gasps, I thought my glamour had worn off until I looked down and realised that the photo of my mother I'd swiped from the attic wasn't glamoured while the rest of me was. Oops. I dropped down behind a building and turned myself visible again, then strode innocently down the high street as though I'd been there all along.

And then I drew to a stop as I spotted Nathan coming the other way, from the direction of the police station. He halted in front of me. "Hey, Blair. Did you go for an early-morning flight?"

"I may have screwed up," I admitted. "I went to Blythe's old house to look for the Pixie-Glass, but those two fairies I met up with yesterday were looking for it, too. Steve showed up before I could confront them."

"Wait—Blair, it was *you* who broke into Mrs Dailey's house?" he said. "We got a call at the police station earlier. I should let Steve know—"

"Do you think he'd let me get away with breaking and

entering?" I interrupted. "I know, I shouldn't have done it. Blame the pixie. He's the one who led me to believe the Pixie-Glass was in there."

"I know you wouldn't break into someone's house without good reason, Blair," he said. "I did wonder, when Blythe called the office—"

"Did you say *Blythe* called the police?" I frowned. "I wish the pixie had taken me to her instead of leading me to her house. We're not exactly friends, but maybe I could have convinced her to lend me the Pixie-Glass, if she has it."

Blythe was back in town? This was awkward. She wouldn't be thrilled to know about my trespassing on her property, but on the other hand, she deserved to know those two fairies had been intending steal her jailed mother's possessions. Question was, had she ever met them before? It made no sense for them to be there otherwise, unless someone else at the market knew of our history.

"So the pixie came back?" he asked.

"Yeah, but I lost track of him somewhere in the house," I said. "He's been gone for ages, so I assumed he didn't want to carry messages between my dad and me any longer. But then he showed up wanting me to go to Blythe's house, so I assumed he had a good reason for it."

Nathan's expression softened. "I'm sure he did. I won't tell Steve. As long as you didn't leave any evidence behind…"

"I didn't, but I did take this." I withdrew the picture frame from my pocket and showed Nathan the photograph.

His eyes grew wide. "Is that—"

"My mum. I don't have any pictures of her, and this was just lying in the attic, so…" I blinked, my eyes stinging. "Don't ask me why Mrs Dailey kept a picture of her, I have no idea. I didn't find the Pixie-Glass, though. And those two fairies—I don't know if they knew my dad, or if they were just trying to take the Pixie-Glass because it's worth a lot of money. The guy who was at the stall with them might have tipped them off that the last person who bought one was in jail."

Nathan went quiet for a moment. "And the two normals? The ones who were bewitched by goblin brew?"

Right. That's what I'm supposed *to be looking into.* "Yesterday was a big failure on that front. If it turns out those two fairies were responsible, the police might have caught them in the house, but I doubt it."

"No, it doesn't sound like they were interested in normals," he said.

I heaved a sigh. "Realistically, anyone at the market might have been responsible for bewitching the two normals. There's no common ground between them. They weren't even in the same place when it happened."

"They were within walking distance of one another and the market, though, right?" he said.

"Yeah, but it doesn't sound like the goblins were the culprits," I said. "I'd blame that menace of an elf, but it turns out he spent yesterday hiding in a coffee shop while Alissa and the rest of the hospital staff combed the town looking for him."

"So he can't have been responsible for the second victim," he surmised. "That doesn't mean he wasn't involved."

"The other elves don't want to hear it," I said. "They

think the goblins are to blame, and they won't take no for an answer."

"The goblins supplied the goblin brew, at least," he said.

"Yes, but they insist they didn't sell it to any normals, and it's not like I have proof," I said. "And who am I supposed to report them to? The police can't prosecute anyone outside of Fairy Falls, not without…"

"The hunters," he finished, his mouth pressing in a grim line.

I shook my head. "I can't bring them here on purpose."

"Unfortunately, this is an area where hunters would have the expertise," he said. "They cover anywhere outside of a paranormal community, including the market. If we found proof that someone from the market was selling to humans…"

"They'd get shut down." My heart sank. "This isn't the fault of everyone at the market. It's just one or two people. If the Inquisitor gets involved, a lot of people might lose their livelihoods."

And my own freedom might well be in jeopardy if he came to Fairy Falls and found out what I'd learned about his real identity. At the very least, I could say goodbye to any hopes of speaking to my dad again.

"We don't need to call any of the higher-ups from the hunters," he said. "You're forgetting we have three ex-hunters in town already."

"You, Erin and Buck," I said. "What do you want to do, then?"

"I'll have to think," he said. "Being a fairy, Buck can get more information from the market than Erin can… and if we expose the proof in front of everyone else, they'll collectively kick out the people responsible. We won't need to bring in the hunters."

"Good," I said. "Because if they show up, I won't be able to speak to my dad, with or without a Pixie-Glass."

I couldn't help feeling like I'd screwed up by mentioning my dad at the market in the first place, but he was the one who'd told me to look for the Pixie-Glass and he hadn't mentioned if any of the fairies knew his identity or not. Besides, I hadn't told anyone he was in jail, and they'd never guess what I wanted to use the Pixie-Glass for. Right?

As for those two fairies, if they'd escaped Steve, their next target would be the market, assuming they hadn't left town while they had the chance. As for Blythe? For all I knew, she was at the market, too, though I couldn't picture letting her hair down and dancing with the fairies. It was weird enough that two of them had tried to rob her house on the same morning she'd come back to town.

Whatever the case, I had to expose whoever was responsible for bewitching people outside the paranormal community, before the backlash hit the whole market—and Fairy Falls by extension.

12

Nathan and I met up with Erin and Buck at Charms & Caffeine, where we all bought extra-large coffees in preparation for the day. I figured Layla could use the extra business, considering everyone in town seemed to be sleeping off their hangovers from another late-night session of dancing with the fairies.

"Is there a reason you dragged us out here on our day off, Blair?" Erin winked at me. "Joking, joking. What do you need my help with?"

"It's about those two normals," I explained. "We think they were exposed to goblin brew or something stronger, and while we can't say for sure if the market was involved, we'd rather solve the case before word spreads beyond the town."

"You mean before the hunters find out?" said Erin. "None of us has said a word, don't worry."

"Nathan told me that if the crime is committed outside

of any magical community, it falls to the hunters by default," I explained. "Needless to say, I'd rather solve it before it comes to that."

"So you think someone from the market handed out goblin brew to the humans," Buck said. "And then lied about it."

"I think it was more than goblin brew," I admitted. "I'm told goblin fruit has a stronger effect than the brew does, and the first victim was addled for days. I'm also told nobody sells it at the market, but the second victim gave a description that might have belonged to a fairy."

"A fairy." Erin's eyes rounded. "Oh. So you want to find them before..."

"Before the rest of us take the blame." The two who'd broken into Blythe's house were my prime suspects, but as long as they remained hidden by glamour, they might be anywhere. If the market was their home, they'd end up back there eventually, but I'd need to be sneaky if I wanted to catch them before they fled.

It'd also help if I could find Blythe and explain the situation so I'd have one more person on my team, but she couldn't see through fairy glamour. Only Buck and I shared that talent, and it might not be enough to pin down a couple of fairies who really didn't want to be found.

"There's also that elf, Thistle," Nathan put in. "Want me to watch him?"

"Sure." Thistle had never used glamour, as far as I'd seen, so Nathan would stand more of a chance of keeping an eye on him than on the fairies. "Um, maybe don't tell Steve. Is he still chasing those... suspects?"

"It sounds like he lost track of them." The reassurance in his gaze indicated he wouldn't give me away in front of the others. But did that mean the two fairies had escaped town? "I have teams watching the borders, but when it comes to the market, it's hard to keep track of who's coming and going."

Especially when a not-insignificant proportion of the market's folk could fly *and* glamour themselves invisible. Still, the two fairies weren't from this town, and likely wouldn't go far from the market. I had to find a way to lure them out. And that meant making use of my newfound talent.

A nagging worry in the pit of my stomach told me that I might be too late to contact my dad, whether the hunters showed up or not. The pixie had vanished along with the fairies, and I wouldn't blame him for going back into hiding.

"Then what should we do?" asked Erin. "Snoop around the market and try to catch them out?"

I nodded. "Buck and I can both see through glamour, and use it, too."

Buck looked startled. "I can't use glamour. I've never tried."

"You can't?" I asked. "But… you're wearing one right now. Granted, so am I, but it was my dad who put it on me to start off with."

"Same," he said. "I've never been able to turn invisible or anything. Never had anyone to teach me."

Huh. "I'd have thought it'd come in handy in your line of work."

"Nah, the hunters don't do stealth," said Erin. "We're

supposed to kick the door in, not slink around in the shadows."

"Just do this." I demonstrated, snapping my fingers and transforming myself into fairy mode. "The only advice I have is to keep trying, keep focusing until you get it."

I decided to save my newest trick until later—namely, using glamour to make myself look like someone else. I wasn't incredibly confident in my abilities even after all the practise I'd had, in truth, but if it came down to it, perhaps I'd need to wear someone else's face in order to get the answers I was looking for.

Still, from the way Buck's face furrowed in concentration when he snapped his fingers, I wasn't the only fairy who was behind on learning to use magic. I'd been imagining the hunters hiring a crack team of fairies with superpowers, but Buck had put that assumption to rest. No matter how many times he snapped his fingers, there was no change.

"Maybe use your other hand?" I suggested.

"Why would it work any different with my other hand?" he wanted to know.

"It does for me. Something about being half witch and half fairy. My wand only works properly in my other hand." I gave another demonstration, snapping the fingers of my right hand.

Wearing a sceptical expression, he gave a snap of his fingers. This time, wings extended behind his shoulders, and his ears turned pointy. His blond hair lightened until it appeared almost silver, while his skin gained an odd glowing sheen.

"Great job," I said.

Erin gawked at him. "Wow."

Buck hesitated. "You don't like it?"

"No, I love it. You still look like you, just… different." Erin grinned. "I like the wings. Are you going to fly?"

He blinked. "I've never flown in my life. Is now really a good time to start learning?"

"Yes, it is," Erin said. "We don't want the hunters coming here and ruining our fun. We moved to Fairy Falls to get away from them."

"I know we did," said Buck. "This is going to be weird, but I'll give it a go."

"I'll be in town if you need me," Nathan said. "Just shoot me a text and I'll be there."

"Sure thing. Good luck with the elf."

Nathan and I parted ways with a kiss, and then Erin, Buck and I headed for the path leading outside the town.

The market was just opening for the day, already bustling with elves and goblins setting up their stalls. Turning invisible, I watched the goblins' stall for a moment, though I didn't really expect to see anything suspicious. Then I looked for the fairies, but their stall wasn't there, and there was no sign of the male fairy who'd spoken to me before. Maybe they'd all left the town together.

I approached an elf at a nearby stall selling jewellery. "Excuse me, do you know where the two fairies, Holly and Heather, are?"

"Those two?" she said. "They went home."

No, they didn't. They went to rob Blythe's house. "What about Dill?"

"Haven't seen him. People come and go all the time at the market."

True. She didn't know about the robbery, and if the

three of them hadn't told anyone where they were going, even my lie-sensing power wouldn't be able to find them.

Heart sinking, I moved to the next stall and received a similar non-answer. I needed to try another tactic. Most people were reluctant to speak to me even as a fairy, so perhaps I'd get on better if I pretended to be one of them.

It was time to test drive my new talent.

I flew the short distance downhill to the lake, where I turned visible again. Then I snapped my fingers and pictured one of the elves I'd seen at the market earlier. To my own surprise, it worked on the first go, and when I peered at my reflection in the lake, I startled at the sight of a short pointy-eared creature standing in my place.

Then I spotted two other elves sleeping in the shallows by the lake. It was a wonder the freezing water hadn't woken them up, but they looked vaguely familiar to me. Hang on… they were the same elves Bramble and Twig had chased off. Hadn't they learned their lesson from the last time they'd drunkenly wandered close to the lake?

"Hey," I called to them. "Hey! Wake up."

One of the elves cracked an eye open. "Are you the elf king?"

"Sure, why not," I said, imitating Bramble's growly voice. "I wish to find two fairies. How would I go about tracking them down?"

"We don't talk to the fairies," mumbled the elf. "They're tricky, they are."

"They are?" That was news to me. "I thought it was goblins you didn't like."

"The goblins give us brew, and so we like them," said the second elf, lifting his head from the water.

Hmm. "Have you ever tried goblin fruit?"

"Do you think we have a death wish?" He laughed, as though I'd told a hilarious joke. "Deadly poison to us, isn't it?"

"Deadly poison?" My heart jolted in my chest. "You mean to elves?"

"What else would I mean?" He pushed upright, then toppled back over into the water. "You're awfully slow for a king."

Time to go, I think. So goblin fruit was poisonous to elves? That meant Thistle couldn't have been the one who'd given it out, unless he hadn't eaten the fruit himself before giving it to those two normals. But that didn't seem right, either.

I left the elves snoring in the shallows and retreated into the woods to remove my disguise without being spotted. Not that the elves were paying the slightest bit of attention. *Deadly poison?* His words had carried a ring of truth I couldn't deny.

I debated heading back to the market disguised as an elf, but I had a better idea. I pictured one of the two fairies from Blythe's house and then snapped my fingers. Then, making sure not to fly too close to the elves, I returned to the lake to check my reflection.

A stranger looked back at me. I looked so much like Heather that I actually had to turn and check she wasn't behind me. *Calm down, Blair.* As long as the real fairy didn't show up in the middle of my investigation, I might be able to pull this off.

"You're still in town?" said a voice.

I rotated on the spot, finding the two elves had dragged themselves out of the water and crept up behind me. *They didn't see me transform, did they?* From their cross-eyed expressions, they were too addled to see their own feet, so I nodded. "Yep. Still in town. That's me."

I tried to make my voice go higher in imitation of the fairy, but I sounded more like I'd inhaled helium.

The elf sat down in the shallows, while his companion dozed against the bank. "Thought you were making a run for it with your sister."

Huh? "I said that, did I?"

He gave a vigorous nod. "You just did. Didn't she?"

His companion grunted in agreement.

Perhaps the fairies hadn't been as secretive about their mission as I'd assumed. "Yes, I'm leaving now… bye."

I flew back uphill to the market, which had officially opened to the public for the day. Witches, shifters and elves roamed among the stalls, picking up trinkets and sipping from mugs of goblin brew. I fluttered my wings, tossed my hair back as I'd seen the fairies do, but I hadn't spent enough time observing Heather to copy her mannerisms directly. And anyone might see through my glamour if they had a strong enough ability. I needed to avoid drawing too much attention.

My gaze fell on the stall selling goblin fruit seeds. They were the closest thing here to actual goblin fruit, so perhaps the goblin at the stall knew something. Right now, she was talking to a witch wearing a green hat. Argyle Winthrop. The gardener witch who'd got herself injured in her own flowerbed.

Treading carefully, I leaned forward to listen to their conversation, and caught the word, "Please."

"No," said the goblin. "We don't deal in that stuff."

"It's urgent," Argyle insisted. "Please."

I fluttered closer, and a shout cut through the air from elsewhere in the market.

"Hunters!" yelled a voice.

Hunters.

They're here.

Pandemonium broke out. Elves, humans and goblins alike fled the market or hid behind their stalls. My wings beat, caught up in the chaos, but I had nowhere to fly. Both ways in and out of the market were blocked, and the hunters marched into view, starkly human among the magic and wonder.

"We got a tip-off that someone here was bewitching humans," one of them said in a loud, carrying voice. "Anyone want to confess?"

Who told them? Nobody from Fairy Falls *wanted* them to come here. Not even Buck and Erin, surely. Or Nathan.

Speaking of whom… I recognised him leading another group of people through the market towards the hunters. Fairy Falls's security team was on the case, and soon enough, they had the hunters surrounded. From Nathan's body language, he was telling them to clear off, but now they'd trekked all the way here, I doubted they'd leave without a fuss.

I have to do something. If I'd caught the person responsible for bewitching the normals early enough, I might have been able to prevent any of this, but I was operating on entirely too little information. The elves had been right to be worried. Not only had I failed to find the culprit, but the last people I wanted in town were back here and stirring up trouble. *Please, please don't let them have brought the Inquisitor along, too.*

Someone caught my arm, an elf leaning closer to me. "You shouldn't be here."

"I—" Crap. I wasn't Blair. They thought I was Heather. Or Holly. I'd forgotten which was which. "Why shouldn't I?"

"You betrayed us," hissed the elf. "You brought them here."

I swivelled, spotting two hunters heading my way. In a swift beat of my wings, I launched myself behind the nearest stall and snapped my fingers to remove my disguise. Then I turned into my human form, crouching out of sight.

A fluttering noise prompted me to turn around, and I spotted two winged figures flitting across the distant hillside.

Can that be them?

One way to find out. Turning into my fairy mode once more, I took flight over the rolling hills and landed in front of Heather and Holly. "Where are you two going?"

"Where else?" one of them said. "We're leaving. We're not staying here with the hunters prowling around the market."

"You wanted to steal the Pixie-Glass," I reminded them. "Did you really think the stunt you pulled at Mrs Dailey's house wouldn't draw their attention?"

"I didn't know she was with—them." Holly shuddered.

True.

"Then why break into her house to begin with?" I asked, baffled. "To get the Pixie-Glass and sell it? You weren't exactly stealthy about it."

"We didn't think there was anyone home," Heather insisted. "He told us—"

"Dill," I said. "He told you to steal it for him. Right?"

Holly's shoulders slumped. "Yeah, we steal things for Dill. So what? We're allowed to earn a living. Not much else people like us can do in this world. We can't all pretend to be human like you do."

I opened and closed my mouth. I had no idea what life was like for the fairies, not really, because I spent most of my days walking around as a human. If I hadn't been a witch on my human side, I might have been recruited to the hunters like Buck—or, if my dad hadn't put the glamour on me, I might have ended up out on the streets.

The two fairies turned their backs on me and vanished in a shower of glitter. I took a step after them, but another shout prompted me to turn back to the market. I snapped my fingers to turn invisible, taking to the skies again. The other fairies had disappeared from sight, and if they *were* the culprits, I could say goodbye to any chance I might have had of quietly handing them over to the police.

Not to mention I'd lost my shot at getting my hands on the Pixie-Glass. How was I supposed to contact my dad with the very people who'd jailed him back in town?

I skidded to a halt in mid-air. Below me, Nathan's security team continued to argue with the hunters, but another person had joined them. *Blythe.*

Silent and invisible, I flew overhead to listen to them.

"Look, it was a mistake," Blythe was saying to one of the hunters. "I don't know who broke into my house, but that's no reason for you people to be here. Who called you?"

Hang on. Blythe *hadn't* been the one who'd called the hunters?

"We had orders," said one of the hunters. "We were

told to come here if anyone broke into your mother's house."

Mrs Dailey must have had people watching the place. But they couldn't have seen me go in there, surely, because I'd been invisible almost the entire time. Except when I'd confronted the fairies… who'd claimed not to know Mrs Dailey had been involved with the hunters.

The question was, what had happened to Dill, the third fairy in their group, and the one who'd sent them to steal the Pixie-Glass?

"I didn't call you," said Blythe. "Technically, the house is mine, and I'm telling you to leave town."

"No, it isn't," said the hunter. "It belongs to your mother, and she requested that we let her know if anyone trespasses on her property during her absence."

What? She must have given the orders before she'd been hauled off to jail, surely… but that didn't stop me from looking wildly around in case Mrs Dailey was hiding among the market stalls all the same.

"Nobody stole anything," Blythe said. "I checked. Maybe my sister went in to get some stuff from in her old room."

Had she not noticed the picture from the attic was missing? Or was she covering for me, knowing the picture was of my mother? I had no idea anymore. All I knew was that by going to her house, I'd drawn the hunters here. And now the Inquisitor was one step closer to guessing that I was on the lookout for the Pixie-Glass. Once he figured that out, he'd know I was trying to contact my dad.

The rest of the hunters all but ignored Nathan and the security team as they prowled through the market, peering into each tent and behind each stall as though looking for wrongdoers. All of them looked to be human rather than fairies, but that didn't put me at ease. They weren't supposed to be in town. And really, if anyone needed to lighten up and join in the fairies' party, it was the hunters. Maybe I could invisibly drop some goblin brew on their heads, but I somehow doubted that'd improve the situation.

A sudden gust of wind caught my wings, sending me flipping over in mid-air. I raised my head to see several dark shapes in the sky, drawing closer. A moment later, Steve and two of his fellow gargoyles landed in front of the hunters.

"What are you doing here?" he demanded. "Get out of our town."

"We had a tip-off that someone was stirring up trouble at the market," said one of the hunters. "It sounds like your security team took on more than they could handle."

"Nonsense," Steve snapped. "We have more than enough people to police our town, and we were doing a fine job of it before you barged in. Go away."

Since when did Steve praise Nathan? Since the two of them were set against the hunters, I'd guess. It made a welcome change from his usual attitude, but the hunters didn't budge an inch.

"Your town is still on our list as a known haunt for troublemakers," said the hunter, "which requires us to step in whenever you make decisions that put the secrecy of the magical community at risk."

"We already passed your inspection," Steve insisted. "You were supposed to leave us alone. That was part of the deal."

"Not all of you," he said. "Not as long as you still harbour the offspring of a criminal."

A criminal?

They must mean me.

The hunters—and the Inspector—were still watching me. They'd been watching me all along, waiting for me to slip up and give them an excuse to come back.

13

I flew over the fields and back into Fairy Falls. Shame trailed after me, urging me to turn back, but showing my face would only make the situation worse. The hunters had confirmed my fear: they'd been watching the whole town because of me. Because of my dad.

I'd made things even worse by breaking into Mrs Dailey's house, but then again, even if I hadn't followed the pixie, those two fairies would still have tried to break in and drawn the hunters' attention. Except they'd been there because my own words had tipped them off to Mrs Dailey buying the Pixie-Glass. No matter how I looked at it, I'd screwed up. And now my two major suspects had flown out of town, leaving the rest of the market to take the fall for their crimes.

As for the third suspect? No sign of him. I kept an eye out for any signs of wayward fairies in town, and spotted Erin and Buck walking away from the market.

Turning visible again, I landed beside them. Erin

jumped at the sight of me, but Buck didn't. He'd turned back into his human form, without so much as a wing in sight.

"You left?" I asked.

"Well, yeah." Buck shuffled his feet, looking embarrassed. "I forgot how to turn into my human form, and I wasn't gonna show my face in front of the hunters with the wings out."

"You're forgetting some of your fellow hunters also have wings," I reminded him. "Not the ones they sent today, though." It didn't really matter in the end. Fairies or human, they were still hunters, after all.

"How'd they know to come here to begin with?" asked Erin. "My brother said they weren't watching the town any longer. I'm glad they didn't send my older brothers, at least. Or my dad."

"No, they shouldn't be here," I said. "It's… kind of my fault they came. Long story short, I went looking around someone's house I shouldn't have been at, and they raised the alarm."

"Whose house?" Erin said.

"Mrs Dailey, Blythe's mother." My face heated. "I found out at the market that she might have something I need pretty badly, and since she's in jail, I wondered if she'd left it behind. I'd have asked her daughter, but she was out of town…"

"So you broke into her house." Erin cracked a grin. "You're more of a rebel than I gave you credit for."

"I wouldn't have done it if it hadn't been urgent." I shook my head. "I need it to contact my dad, but I didn't count on those two fairies getting the same idea. They— the two fairies from the market—I'm sure they're the ones who bewitched those two humans as well as breaking into Mrs Dailey's house and raising the alarm."

"Did you say contact your dad?" said Buck. "Isn't he in jail?"

"There's no other way." From the disbelieving expression on his face, I'd made a mistake in mentioning it in front of him. "I'm ninety percent sure he was set up anyway and shouldn't be there, but I've never met him in person and I just wanted to talk to him."

Buck's expression turned frosty. "Okay, whatever you're planning, I want nothing to do with it. I'm not going to get on the hunters' bad side, not now I'm finally shot of them."

He walked away. Erin shot me an apologetic look and hurried after him.

Tears of frustration stung my eyes. Why had I decided to open my big mouth? I should have flown after those two fairies myself, but without knowing where they'd gone, I'd be doing nothing but painting a target on my own head. Still, why had I thought confiding in someone who'd only just left the hunters would do anything other than backfire on me?

Going home was out of the question, so I found myself wandering down the high street instead. I went inside the hospital, out of any other ideas, and waited in the lobby until Alissa came out of a nearby ward.

"What's wrong, Blair?" asked Alissa.

"Everything," I said. "The *hunters* found out about the two humans and now they're marching around the market, terrorising everyone."

"Seriously?" Her brows shot up. "Why'd someone call them?"

"I may have broken into Blythe's house."

She listened to my account of the day's misadventures. When I'd finished, she said, "It's not your fault the hunters showed up. They were looking for an excuse to."

"And I gave them one." I winced. "Why didn't I guess Mrs Dailey would have had someone watching her house? She must have figured I'd come snooping around eventually. As for the hunters... *I'm* the reason they're still watching the town. Now the whole market is in trouble and probably Fairy Falls, too."

The market was a convenient scapegoat, but for all I knew, they wanted Fairy Falls as a whole to take the blame for whoever was bewitching humans. If they got to take over the town, too, all the better.

Alissa shook her head. "I think the hunters would have come to town again no matter what. We couldn't keep this case quiet forever, not as long as normals are still being affected."

"What's going on with Spud, then?" I asked.

"He's almost fully recovered," she said. "Stopped babbling about wings, too. I think the hallucinations have worn off."

"Oh, good." At least someone's day was looking up, because things looked pretty bleak for the rest of us. "I'm sure Thistle wasn't involved after all, given that goblin fruit is deadly poison to elves like him. I reckon he's probably safe from taking the blame, but the hunters have planted themselves in the market and are refusing to leave."

"What are they doing, looking for the culprit?" she asked.

"They were arguing with Steve last I checked," I said.

"And Blythe. She didn't call them, it turns out, and she wasn't happy about them being here."

"I wonder who did." Her forehead scrunched up. "I guess Mrs Dailey might have had a security spell somewhere in her house that went off when you flew in. I'm surprised that pixie didn't consider the possibility."

"Unless it was those two fairies who tripped the alarm." I thought back. "They were completely inept at stealth and nearly got us all caught, but they bolted for it as soon as the hunters showed up at the market. If they hadn't, I'd have hauled them over to the police."

Alissa's breath caught. "Oh, Spud—you're not supposed to be out here."

The second victim of the goblin brew stood in the doorway, barefoot and dishevelled. I didn't know how much of our conversation he'd heard, but he didn't look as freaked out as he had last time we'd seen one another. He gave me a wary look. "I remember you, but you're different this time. No wings."

So it was true—his sight had faded, and he couldn't see through my glamour any longer. "Hey," I said. "See, we're not monsters. Do you remember anything more about where it started?"

"Everyone keeps asking me that," he said. "I remember my car broke down in a field, and I was walking along looking for help. The next thing I remember is running around surrounded by... like, winged monsters."

"So someone gave you the drug in the field?" Alissa gave me a nudge, which I gathered to mean meant that was the cover story they'd gone with.

"I guess they did," he said. "What kind of hospital is this, by the way? When do I leave?"

"Soon," Alissa said. "We just need to fill out some more paperwork first. Go back to your ward, and I'll be with you in a minute."

I watched him leave. "He seems a lot better."

"Told you," said Alissa. "I reckon that idiot elf gave the first guy one of his cocktails and lied about it. That's why it took Riff so much longer to recover."

I dragged my gaze from the door. "It sounds like Spud was wandering around the fields alone when he ended up falling under the spell. Like Riff, someone gave him the goblin fruit out there. It didn't happen in the normal world. It happened in the field, somewhere between here and Sloan."

The sound of someone clearing their throat came from behind a potted plant. A head popped out, wearing a purple wig with a wand tucked behind her ear. Old Ava, the seer... and *she'd* definitely heard every word of our conversation.

"Hello, Briar," she said.

"It's Blair," I said. "Hey, Ava. Were you eavesdropping on us?"

"You shouldn't be out of your room," said Alissa.

"I need to talk to Briar," she insisted. "I need to tell you that if you intend to walk in the hills, watch out for the winged one."

"The winged one?" I said blankly. "Was that one of your seer's visions? Who do you mean? One of the fairies?"

Alissa moved towards her, but the old seer was already sauntering away, back towards her room. "Don't give up, Briar. Your mother will be proud of you."

Her words would have had more impact if she'd got

my name right. "I think the goblin fruit is rubbing off on all of us."

"Nah, that's just Ava." Alissa rolled her eyes. "If I didn't know better, I'd say that elf put the spirit of rebellion into all the other patients."

"At least she didn't try to leave." It was beyond me to tell what she'd been warning me about, but maybe... maybe she'd had a point about my mother. Tanith Wildflower had gone so far as to steal the Head Witch's sceptre and risk arrest in order to keep me safe. I'd always thought of her as far braver than I was, but I'd do the same for the people I cared about.

If I didn't confront the hunters head-on, if I didn't get rid of them before the Inquisitor came back to join them here in Fairy Falls, then they'd do the same to the people at the market as they'd done to my dad. They didn't care if the person they caught was innocent or not.

There was one thing for it: I needed to find the place where the two normals had been ensnared. The place, no doubt, where those fairies had fled to.

And there was one person remaining in town who might know where it was.

14

I left the hospital, a fresh wave of resolve guiding my steps as I veered towards the Laughing Pixie.

As I'd suspected, I found Thistle the elf sitting at a table in the corner of the pub, a neon blue cocktail on the table in front of him. No other customers were present. Everyone must be at the market.

Pix stood behind the bar, and when she saw me, she gave me a nod of acknowledgement. "Want a drink?"

"Why do you play along with him?" I asked.

"He gives great tips," she admitted. "I need the money. Anyway, he's happy enough here."

I approached the elf and gave him a prod in the shoulder. "Hey," I said. "I need to ask you a question."

He slid off the stool into a heap on the floor, then scrambled to his feet and tried to run out of the pub.

Before he could move an inch, I snagged the elf's arm. "Tell me," I said. "Did you give the goblin brew to anyone else? Who paid you off?"

"I didn't!" he said. "I gave it to the first human, yes, but

I was not the person who caused him to fall under the spell to begin with, not at all."

"And it's a coincidence that you were walking around drunkenly on the same high street where the second victim showed up a day later?" I said. "Don't deny it—you know where the goblin fruit is. Don't you?"

"Goblin fruit?" said Pix.

"Those two humans were under the influence of more than just goblin brew," I explained. "Now the hunters are rampaging through the market and ready to take over the town as they planned to, and innocent people will end up getting caught in the aftermath unless I find the real culprit. The whole town will."

"Is there anything I can do to help?" she said. "I don't want the hunters coming here either."

"They're already here." I turned to Thistle. "I just want to know where the fruit is. The goblin fruit. I know you went wandering in the hills, and you found it, even if you didn't eat it yourself. Right?"

"I may have gone for a wander in the hills," he said. "And I happened upon a wondrous grove of seven oak trees in a circle. In the centre, a tree grew, like a small miracle. Pity the fruit is poison to my kind… but it would have been easy for any human lost in the hills to stumble across it."

Especially if a fairy had led them astray.

"Thanks." I got to my feet. "That's all I wanted to know."

Now all I had to do was find the tree and then lead the hunters to it. The slight issue, of course, was that I was short on a few allies. Nathan had taken it upon himself to stall the hunters single-handedly, and Erin and Buck were gone. Which left…

"Sky," I said aloud. "I need you."

A moment passed. A *long* moment. I kept walking, then launched into flight towards the lake. Had Sky stayed at the market and got caught up with the hunters—or was he still with the other fairy cats? He hadn't ditched me at a time like this, had he?

"Miaow." I flew uphill towards the sound of a chorus of meowing, relief flooding me. Sky stood waiting on the path, the other fairy cats gathering around him. *Of course he didn't ditch me.*

I landed in front of him. "Sky, can you do me a favour? I'm going to find the source of the goblin fruit the two normals ate, but the hunters won't take my word for it. I need someone to bring them to the source. With any luck, that's where the fairies are hiding, too."

"Miaow," he said. I took that to mean, *leave that to me.*

"Thanks, Sky." I dropped down to give him a stroke, and he padded off, leading his troop of new friends.

Snapping my fingers to turn invisible, I took flight once more over the hillside. The hunters had gathered in a cluster outside the market, arguing with the town's security team. From the looks of things, they had no intention of leaving now they'd found another excuse to drag Fairy Falls's name through the mud.

If I brought them to the real culprits, they might finally agree to leave Fairy Falls alone, but there were no guarantees. They probably wouldn't take kindly to being herded by a flock of fairy cats, either, but I was all out of other ideas as to how to get them to look for the source of the trouble.

I kept flying, looking for any signs of the trees that Thistle had described. After circling the hills a half-dozen times, I wondered if he'd been having me on—then I spotted a small copse of trees nestled between two hills. I counted seven oak trees, and a number of round golden fruits hung from the branches of a smaller tree in the centre of the oaks. *There it is.*

I landed in front of the tree, unsure of my options. Could I just yank it up by the roots? If the hunters refused to follow Sky and the other cats, I'd have to bring the proof directly to them, but the tree was as tall as I was, and each of the fruits was almost as big as my head.

I reached for the branches, trying to get a grip on the lowest fruit.

"Leave my tree alone," said a voice.

I turned on the spot. The gardener witch, Argyle Winthrop, stood there with a wand in her hand.

"So it's yours?" The fairies *weren't* responsible? "Did you plant it? You grew this tree in a place exposed to normals on purpose? Why?"

"No." She lowered her wand. "It was an accident. Someone gave me some seeds, and I dumped them in a nearby field. Later on, I went looking for them, only to find they'd grown in my absence."

Not a word she spoke was a lie, but I hadn't been prepared to deal with a witch instead of a group of fairies, and I'd come here expecting to find someone who was definitely guilty of a crime. I hadn't a clue how the paranormal laws would react to someone accidentally growing a tree of intoxicating fruit, but I'd bet the hunters would take no excuses. And where, then, were the fairies?

"Couldn't you have moved the tree before it grew this

big?" I asked. "Two normals have already found their way here, and if you don't tell the authorities it exists, the market will get into a lot of trouble."

"They'd deserve it." She sniffed. "That goblin does. She refused to deal with me. Said she wouldn't buy the seeds. Then I tried to sell her the fruit and she wouldn't buy that, either."

"So you weren't buying from her at the market?" I thought I'd seen her pleading to buy the fruit, but I hadn't heard most of their conversation. "You were trying to sell the tree? Or just the fruit?"

"Look, I needed the money," she said. "If it wasn't impossible for me to legally sell the seeds to anyone, I wouldn't have thrown them out and we wouldn't be having this conversation."

"Even so, it's not legal for the tree to stay this far away from any paranormal community," I told her. "Besides, at this rate, the hunters will shut the market down and you'll have no chance of ever selling that fruit to anyone. They'll take away the tree, cut it down, and probably lock you in jail, too."

Her face crumpled. "I can't—I can't leave it. It's all I've got."

I shook my head. "The hunters are already on their way here. I thought those fairies were responsible, but I guess they must have hidden themselves away."

I hadn't seen anything in the tree, but who knew, maybe they were lurking nearby all the same. I wheeled around, scanning my surroundings, and recoiled in shock.

A pile of bushes nearby nearly concealed several bodies—several *living* bodies. Not fairies, but humans.

My foster parents. Ropes bound their hands and feet,

cloths muffled their cries, and their expressions were glazed. I didn't stop to think before pulling out my wand and flicking it, removing Mrs Wilkes's gag, then Mr Wilkes's.

The two of them cringed backwards into the bushes, looking at me in horror.

"Wings," whispered Mrs Wilkes. "She has wings."

They were under the effects of goblin fruit.

15

I spun back to Argyle. "You kidnapped my parents and force-fed them goblin fruit? *Why?*"

"No!" She paled, staring into the bushes at the two captive humans. "No, I didn't see them there. I ran all the way back here from the market to check on my tree when the hunters showed up. I swear, I didn't see a single person anywhere."

True. But that meant… *They were glamoured before she got here. The fairies left them here.*

"Monsters!" yelled Mr Wilkes in alarm, pointing at me.

My heart contracted. Both he and my foster mother shrank away into the bushes, their expressions terror-stricken. Tears stung my eyes. "I'm not a monster, I'm your daughter."

How could this be possible? If they were glamoured, then someone else had hidden them from view. Someone like… a certain pair of fairies. They *must* be close enough to see the tree. Which meant they'd heard every word we said.

I rotated on the spot, squinting around for any more signs of hidden glamours. "Who else is out there? Show yourselves."

When no response came, I raised my wand and fired off a warning shot of glitter. At once, the two fairies from the market descended in a gleam of wings and light.

"You," I said. "I knew you were involved."

"We didn't glamour them." Holly looked down at my foster parents with wide, frightened eyes. "Not us."

Truth. But then… who?

A third flash of light heralded the arrival of Dill… and he held a wand in his hand. Magic crackled off the end, raising the hairs on my arms.

"You?" I said. "I don't understand. You helped me."

"Yes, I did." He pointed his wand at me, looking almost sad. "Before I realised who you were, and who your father was. You should have stayed away from the market, Blair."

Rustling sounded as the other two fairies each drew a long wooden stick. *Fairies with wands.* How was that possible? Yet that hardly mattered, considering what Dill had just said.

"You knew my dad?"

"I wish I hadn't." Dill's eyes turned cold. "He betrayed us when he chose that witch over his own people."

"*You* lured the hunters to town," I said. "You did, didn't you? You bewitched those two normals, and when that didn't work, you sent Holly and Heather to steal from that house and then told tales on them in the hopes that the hunters would come here."

The two fairies gave each other uncertain looks. "You're lying."

Dill wore a calm expression. "Your people drove us out

of the magical world at large. The witches did. Just look at this town of yours. Fairy Falls, it's called, and not a single fairy in sight."

"I *am* a fairy," I said heatedly. "Besides, why the hunters? They're not going to make things any better for you."

"I beg to differ," he said. "They'll remove this witch council of yours and allow us to take back what is ours. And you, Blair, will not stand in our way this time."

This time. He was with the Inquisitor. Raw fear pounded in my chest. The hunters might make things better for the other fairies if they were in power, for all I knew, but the other paranormals would pay the price for it, I was certain. And I couldn't let them take my home away.

A gasp came from the bushes. I stole a glance behind me. Mr and Mrs Wilkes clung to each other, looking at the three fairies in terror. With the true sight, they saw it all.

Behind me, Argyle was looking between us, her body frozen. Her wand still in her hand. I gave her a pleading look, but she didn't move, too frightened to budge an inch. I couldn't take on three fairies alone. Especially with my foster parents hiding in the bushes, thinking I was a stranger. Thinking I was a monster.

I looked back at him. "Please, whatever you want with me, leave my parents out of this. They have nothing to do with the witches, the fairies… anything."

"I will gladly let them go, if you promise to leave this world and never come back," he said.

"Are you kidding me?" I'd thought the hunters wanted

to recruit me, not kick me out. "I won't leave Fairy Falls. This is my home. More than it is yours."

"It *was* my home." Dill raised his wand, and a jet of sparks shot towards me. I took to the air, my wings beating, but I didn't dare fly out of range of my foster parents in case he hurt them.

"What did I ever do to you?" I yelled over my shoulder. "And my foster parents? They don't even know fairies exist. Or they didn't."

I flew in circles as I talked, dodging another spell, but even conjuring a shower of glitter didn't bring anyone running to help. I'd flown too far away, out of sight of Fairy Falls, and it didn't look as though the cats and the hunters were coming to help me after all.

Dill flicked his wand, sending a jet of air at me. I flew head over heels, crashing into the sprawling branches of the tree. Grabbing one of the goblin fruits, I tugged at the branch, hard. Argyle's hands grabbed mine and helped me give one last firm tug. The fruit broke free, and I flung it into Dill's face.

The fruit exploded. Yellow pulp splattered his face, seeds flew left and right. Dill gave a bellow of rage and waved his wand, and this time, I had nowhere to run. I grabbed my own wand and waved it in a zigzag motion.

I didn't expect it to work on fairy magic, but the shower of sparks bounced off my shield and flew in the other direction. With an anguished shriek, Argyle sprung out from behind the tree and blasted him out of the air.

With a snarl, he raised his wand hand—and Nathan grabbed his arm from behind, holding it behind his back.

Nathan. My heart lifted with relief. Behind him, Sky padded along, leading Erin and Buck... along with a whole pack of fairy cats. I glimpsed more people behind them, but before I could take it all in, Dill twisted out of Nathan's grip, taking aim again.

Sky grew to full size, positioning himself between my foster parents and the three fairies. Several other fairy cats ran up to the clearing, turning into their monster-sized selves, too. The other two fairies still held their wands, but their expressions had turned to fear. They knew no glamour would get them out of this one.

"You're outnumbered now," I warned them. "There's nowhere to run. Or fly."

Dill wiped a handful of goblin fruit from his face and aimed another attack at me, only to miss wildly. His eyes had begun to glaze over.

"You poisoned him!" said one of the other fairies in accusing tones.

"He set you up," I retaliated. "He sent you to burgle that house because he knew it'd alert the hunters. He'd happily throw both of you under the broomstick to get what he wants."

"She's lying!" His words were slurred, while he dropped mid-flight, on a level with the goblin fruit tree.

Argyle flung herself at him, grabbing his feet and pulling him out of the air. As she and the fairy grappled, a jet of light hit both of them, and they fell unconscious to the ground.

I looked around for the caster, and spotted a larger group approaching along the hillside, led by Madame Grey. Backup had arrived, in the form of half the leading witch coven. Gargoyles flew in from above, blocking the fairies' escape route, while more people from the market followed on foot. My heart gave an unwelcome jolt at the sight of the hunters, then relief swept over me when Madame Grey overtook them.

She reached us first, halting beside Dill and the unconscious Argyle. "Would someone like to tell me what's going on here?"

I did my best to, with some input from Nathan. I made sure to stress that while Argyle had been the one who'd dropped the goblin fruit seeds, it was the fairies who were at fault for luring in normals unlucky enough to stray too close when wandering through the fields. I also made it clear that Dill was the instigator, though the other two were far from blameless.

After I'd finished, Madame Grey and the witches moved in to discuss the culprits' punishment with the hunters. I wasn't really a part of that conversation, so I moved to Nathan's side.

"I'm glad you're okay, Blair," he said.

"Same," said Erin, with a guilty look at Buck. We'd need to talk about what I'd told them earlier, but that would have to wait until we didn't have an audience.

"Thanks for coming," I said. "How'd you know where to find me?"

"I saw you flying," said Buck in explanation. "Also, your familiar insisted."

"He's good at that."

"Miaow," said Sky, alerting my attention to the bushes where my foster parents cowered away from the noise. He and the others had turned back to their normal-cat sizes now that the fairies were surrounded, but Mr and Mrs Wilkes both wore expressions of utter terror, and they shrank away when I approached them.

"Who are they?" asked Erin.

"They're my foster parents." I swallowed hard. "They're under—they're under the effects of the goblin fruit. I have to get them out of here, but I don't want to frighten them."

I also didn't want them to see me like this, without glamour, but with the goblin fruit in effect, I didn't have a choice. Both of them cringed away from me when I moved closer.

"Wings."

I flinched. "You know me. I'm Blair. I'm still me. I know I don't look like me, but I am…"

"Blair."

My body tensed. "Do you… do you know who I am?"

My foster parents rose to their feet and moved closer to me. "Blair. You're… different."

I smiled weakly. "I am. But I'm still me. I promise, I'm going to help you."

They knew who I was. They knew I wasn't a monster. And that's all that mattered.

16

M r and Mrs Wilkes took a full day to recover from the effects of the goblin fruit. It could have been much worse, and I was just relieved they'd made it out intact and without any other side effects. The fairies hadn't been so lucky. Dill had to go on trial in front of the gargoyles and a team of hunters with the goblin fruit still in full effect, but I didn't have much sympathy for him, given what he'd done to my family.

The hunters didn't seem to care that he'd been trying to get them to come here intentionally, because he'd still broken the law. His desperate attempt at revenge on the witches had backfired on him, majorly. Not to mention his two companions. Last I'd heard, the hunters and witches had come to an agreement that all three of them would face a long stint in the hunters' jail as well as a hefty fine to be paid to the rest of the market.

I skipped out on their trial, more concerned with

making sure Mr and Mrs Wilkes were okay. Nathan promised to make sure the three fairies weren't let off without punishment, so I left him to handle it and spent the day with my foster parents in the hospital. I told them a little about being half fairy, but I hadn't a clue how much information would stick after the effects of the goblin fruit faded and they forgot their experiences. They might accept me as I really was, for now, but it wasn't safe for them to stay here in Fairy Falls. Not as long as the hunters were watching me.

As I sat in the hospital waiting room between visits, Argyle Winthrop walked in, accompanied by Thistle the elf of all people. The incongruous pair walked towards me, and I sat up straighter, half-expecting Argyle to yell at me for what I'd done to her beloved goblin fruit.

"Um, hi," I said. "Did you fall into a flowerbed again?"

"Not quite," said Argyle. "I just wanted to apologise for fighting you over the tree."

"Don't worry about it." Of everyone involved in the events of the past week, she wasn't even in the top five of the people I was most annoyed with. "I know that fruit is addictive."

"I'm not addicted," she said. "I only tried the brew once, and you saw how that turned out."

"Oh." I frowned. "Then why were you so intent on me not removing the tree?"

"I needed the money." She fiddled with her sleeve. "My shop is a wreck. Falling to pieces. Business has been terrible. I was in a foul mood and hungover when you saw me at the market. Not that that excuses my behaviour, but I saw the tree as the only way I could earn enough cash to fix up my shop."

"What are you doing with Thistle? Did he get injured?" He didn't look it, but he wouldn't meet my eyes.

"He wants to apologise, too, but he's too embarrassed," she said. "Elves and their pride… really."

Was that fondness in her tone? Surely not.

"Apology accepted, then," I said. "All I wanted to do was find the people responsible. And I skipped the trial, so I guess I'll never know why those fairies wanted everyone else at the market to end up suffering the brunt of punishment at the hands of the hunters."

"Actually… we eavesdropped on the trial," Argyle admitted. "It sounded like Dill bullied those two fairies into helping him commit crimes, and tagged along with the market as a cover so people wouldn't get suspicious. All the stuff with the goblin fruit was mostly to get Fairy Falls into trouble, but he claimed he wanted you to be punished, too. Why is he so obsessed with you? Do you know him?"

"Old bit of family history, I guess," I said vaguely.

"Anyway, he tried to talk his way out of being arrested," said Argyle. "Didn't work. I got the impression Steve wanted rid of those fairies *and* the hunters, because he let the hunters carry the prisoners off without arguing that they should be jailed here instead."

Probably for the best, considering. "So they're gone?"

"They left about half an hour ago," she said.

I glanced at the elf, who continued to hover near the door. "Good. I won't miss them."

I wouldn't… and yet it would be a long while before Dill's words left my mind. *Did he really live in Fairy Falls at one time?* And why had he been so angry with me? Because he'd been angry and jealous that I'd been accepted here, while the original fairies had been driven out of town so long ago?

"What about the tree?" I asked Argyle.

"Oh, I have a buyer lined up to pick it up later," she said. "The market staff were very understanding and put me in touch with someone who's legally licenced to sell goblin fruit."

"Good," I said. "And good luck."

The two of them left the hospital waiting room. As they did so, I spotted movement behind a potted plant. Once again, Old Ava was hiding out of sight eavesdropping on people.

"Hey," I said to her. "Let me guess… you don't have permission to leave your room. Again."

"Oh, I wasn't going to miss any of this," she said. "Let my granddaughter have company in her interesting choice of romantic partners."

"They weren't—" I broke off. "Okay, never mind. Anyway, when you told me to be careful, did you know the hunters were coming here?"

"They always follow the call of the fairies," she said. "They can't seem to help it."

I'd always thought she knew more than she let on about my mother, but it was news to me that she knew anything about the hunters' relationship with the fairies. Did she know about the Inquisitor, too?

"But the hunters were the ones who punished them," I said. "The fairies who committed the crimes, I mean."

"Of course they did," she said. "I hear fairies are sticklers for justice. Even against their own."

Justice. If they punished only the guilty, what crimes

had my dad been jailed for? Without the Pixie-Glass, I might never know. Unless…

"Have you ever heard of a Pixie-Glass?" I asked.

"A what?"

"Never mind." She wasn't the person to ask. But I knew who was.

———

The following day, my parents left Fairy Falls. I went to see them off, and while they walked happily with me, they didn't know they were already under the influence of a befuddlement spell which would blur their memories so they'd remember taking a walk with me but not where they'd been or what we'd been doing.

"Lovely place, this," said Mrs Wilkes, as we walked down the cobbled street towards the lake.

"Scenic," her husband put in. "I see why you like it so much, Blair."

"And you're staying here, aren't you?" she asked.

"Yes." My eyes stung with tears. Once the spell kicked in, they'd forget most of this. It was for the best—after all, the hunters' arrival and our near-miss drove home how dangerous the magical world was for normals like them— but I hated lying to them. And I hated that it was necessary.

"It was nice seeing you," Mr Wilkes said to me.

"Thanks, Blair," said Mrs Wilkes.

They knew something wasn't quite right, but they trusted me. And in that instant, when they hugged me goodbye as though I was a little kid again, I knew that I wouldn't be able to fool them forever.

I didn't want to. Someday, I'd find a way to tell them the truth. *I promise I will.*

On my walk back to town, I felt eyes watching me from somewhere nearby. I halted in the middle of the path and spotted a small figure standing behind me. An elf. Not Thistle, but Bramble.

"Blair Wilkes," he said. "You caught the troublemakers who were bewitching humans."

"I did," I said. "The hunters didn't bother you, did they?"

"Our home is too well-hidden for them to find," he said. "The king would speak to you, if you are willing."

"All right." I'd take the elves over the hunters anytime.

We made our way to the forest in silence. Once we reached the elves' territory, I walked after Bramble into the tunnel and into the elf king's domain. As I knelt before him, I realised I'd forgotten to switch out of human mode. To my surprise, however, he didn't comment.

"You found the perpetrator, then," he said.

"I did," I confirmed. "The hunters have left town, and the market will soon follow."

"The hunters should not have come here."

"I think they always planned to." Silence fell between us. I assumed he wanted me to speak, so I added, "But they've left, and they've taken the fairies with them. Did you ever suspect that some of the fairies might want revenge on the witches for taking away their territory? Even to the extent that they'd want the hunters to come into Fairy Falls to drive away the witches?"

This was my home, Dill had said. He believed the witches had driven the fairies off… and now he was in jail, I could only guess at how much truth was in his words. If the hunters were run by fairies, it explained why he'd trust them over the witches.

"No," said the king. "Yet it does not surprise me that some would act against their own interests."

"I mean, some of them work *for* the hunters." Including their leader… but I was starting to suspect few people were aware of that fact, even among the hunters.

"Not your father."

My heart contracted. "Is that why they had him arrested? Or was it because of my mother?"

"I know nothing of the circumstances of your father's arrest, Blair."

True. I heaved a sigh. "I'll be honest, I have no idea which of the fairies are friends or foes these days. Are any of them on my side?"

Even Buck wasn't, though that was more my fault than anything. He hadn't known the backstory on my father and the Inquisitor. But maybe he'd change his mind if I had the chance to explain myself to him.

"That, I cannot say," said the elf king. "Perhaps your father might be able to tell you."

"Yeah, well, that's not happening." A bitter taste filled my mouth. "I didn't find the Pixie-Glass. There wasn't one. Not where I could find it, anyway."

A moment of silence passed. He didn't answer, but he kept watching me as though he wanted me to say something. Was I supposed to condemn the idea of Thistle dating a human? Or had he got over his prejudices in that regard?

"It might interest you to know that I have been informed of where you might obtain a Pixie-Glass," said the elf king. "I had a visitor earlier who was rather distressed, and who told me of your plight."

"Who?" I straightened upright, forgetting about the low ceiling, and hit my head on the earthen surface. Ow. "You know where I can get one? Where?"

"Be patient, Blair Wilkes." He and Bramble exchanged glances. "According to our messenger, it is in the hands of someone for whom you have no liking."

"Someone I don't like… Blythe?" I rubbed my forehead. "Yeah, I know. The pixie took me to her house, but it wasn't there."

"It was he who told me where the Pixie-Glass resides," said the elf king. "At the home of the hunter in charge of the region."

"You mean… you can't mean Nathan's family."

"Yes, Blair."

No way. Nathan's family had a Pixie-Glass? "I can't ask my boyfriend to rob his family."

"Given the right incentive, they might give it to him willingly."

I shook my head. "I seriously doubt it."

My mind reeled. *Nathan's family has a Pixie-Glass.* Not Blythe's mother, and not the Inquisitor. Nathan's dad and brothers weren't my biggest fans and it wouldn't endear me to them if I dragged them into my scheme to contact my father, but for my family's sake, I had to find a way to get hold of that Pixie-Glass.

———

Nathan waited for me on the path leading out of the woods, accompanied by Erin—and Buck.

"Hey," said Nathan, taking my hand. "Did it go well?"

"As well as I might have expected, considering how many times I messed up," I said. "At least he didn't order me to look after Thistle."

That role had gone to Argyle Winthrop. Still, maybe they could help each other. Stranger things had happened.

"So we found our culprit," said Erin. "Or rather, culprits. I like how the whole town comes together in a crisis."

"Yeah, I guess we do." I smiled.

"Sorry about running off," said Buck. "What you said… it was a lot to wrap my head around, and I panicked."

"So did I," I said. "I shouldn't have sprung it on you out of nowhere."

I'd wanted to know at least one fairy was on my side, though if recent events had proven anything, it was that the fairies weren't a united front, to say the least.

"No worries," Buck said. "Like I said—we're cool. I won't sell you out to the hunters. Just to make that clear."

True.

At times like this, I was more grateful for my lie-sensing power than ever.

"Same here," added Erin. "We're with you, Blair. We won't let the hunters lay a finger on you."

I looked between her and Buck. "I have something to tell you, but I'm not exaggerating when I say that if you tell anyone else, it'll put more than our lives in danger."

"Whoa," said Erin. "That sounds pretty serious, but sure, I'm in."

"And me," added Buck.

"Your boss is a fairy," I told her. "Former boss, I mean. And I think he got my family arrested and killed."

Erin and Buck listened, open-mouthed, as I explained what I'd concluded from my conversations with my dad, my mum's ghost, and the various hunters I'd run into. And Blythe, too. She wouldn't be thrilled at me mentioning her name, but given her mother's involvement with the hunters, she had to have known it'd come out eventually.

"The Inquisitor?" Erin shuddered. "I always thought there was something weird about him. Inhuman. But..."

"He's wearing a powerful glamour," I explained. "I don't know what his endgame is, but he got my dad arrested and my mum killed, and there's way too much evidence that he did it on purpose for me to believe my dad was the one in the wrong. Even those three fairies who attacked me yesterday wanted me driven out of town because they thought my dad betrayed the fairies for the witches. Because of my mother."

Buck watched me for a moment. "I can't deny there's something weird about the Inquisitor, but I don't know anything about your dad. I didn't even know he was a fairy. I never worked in the jail."

"So that fairy who attacked you was working with our old boss?" asked Erin.

"No, that's the weird part," I admitted. "Last I saw, the Inquisitor wanted to *recruit* me to work for the hunters. I don't know if he changed his mind or if Dill and the others were acting alone, but I feel like if the Inquisitor wanted to try to hire me again, he'd come back here himself."

Erin shook her head. "Wow, Blair. Okay, that's way too weird for you to have made it all up. Not that I think you did."

"Nah, even I couldn't come up with anything that outlandish," I said. "Anyway, you don't have to commit to anything. I just wanted someone else to know, aside from me and Nathan."

"We're on your team." Erin nudged Buck. "Right?"

He nodded. "Yeah. I won't tell a soul."

True. Nathan took my hand and gave it a reassuring squeeze. "I'm glad you told them."

"I wasn't sure," I murmured. "It feels like I'm setting others up to take the fall if the Inquisitor finds out I know what he is."

He shook his head. "He had to know you'd eventually guess."

"Hmm." I fell into step alongside him as we made our way back towards his house. "I guess so, but it's weird that he tried to recruit me before I knew. Maybe he thought I'd be more useful to him if I was ignorant of what he really was."

And I wasn't, not anymore. I might have endless gaps in my knowledge of all things fairy, but my eyes were wide open. I could thank the market for that, at least.

"Blair?" Nathan squeezed my hand again. "You haven't told me how it went with the elves."

"Oh." Of course I hadn't. "So, it turns out there *is* a Pixie-Glass. The elves asked around and they learned there's one at the local hunters' branch."

"The branch led by my family." Nathan gave a nod of understanding. "You want me to ask my dad if I can borrow it?"

"Would he say yes?"

He shook his head. "I doubt it. He's not best pleased with me at the moment. Nor at Erin. But I'll figure out a way. If you really need this Pixie-Glass… I'll have to make sure he doesn't realise it's for you. I won't put you in danger unnecessarily."

"I know."

But he'd do his best for me. I had no doubts about that. I wasn't alone.

As we neared his house, Sky sat outside the door, waiting for us. I knelt down and gave him a stroke, then turned back to Nathan. "Am I losing my grip, or do you think we have a chance in hell of pulling this off? Of saving my dad and exposing the truth?"

"Only if I am, too." He brushed a kiss to my forehead. "I think we can do this."

"Miaow," Sky said in agreement.

The following day, I went back to my magic lessons. After my successful use of the defensive spell against the fairies, I had enough of a boost in confidence to perform better than I had last time, and both Rebecca and I left the lesson in good spirits.

I'd planned to ask her about her sister, but when we left the classroom, we found Blythe herself standing outside.

Blythe gave me a nod. "Blair."

"Hey," I said. "I guess you figured out what happened at the house."

"It was obvious you were involved, Blair," she said. "I don't care. You can steal everything she owns if you want to."

"I stole a picture of my mum," I admitted. "I take it she didn't want to keep it?"

She blinked. "I didn't even know she had one. I haven't dared touch her stuff in case it's booby-trapped."

"It probably is," I said. "I don't know what tripped the alarm. I was looking for a Pixie-Glass, and the other two people who broke in were looking for the same thing."

"To speak to your dad," she said. "In jail."

"How did you—"

"My mother had the same idea," she said. "She took it with her, in fact."

"She took the Pixie-Glass?" My last hope evaporated into dust. "So it's not at your house. It never was."

"What did you think?" she said. "She wouldn't leave anything that valuable behind, even with her house spelled."

"Who's she using the Pixie-Glass to contact?" I said. "Is she even allowed to have something like that in jail?"

"Don't ask me." She shrugged. "I just figured you'd want to know."

Not a reassuring piece of news. It was bad enough that she and the Inquisitor were in the same place, even if one of them was behind bars. "So there isn't another way to get a Pixie-Glass?"

"No," she said. "Sorry."

Blythe had apologised to me. The world really was ending. I still held hope that Nathan would be able to get hold of the one his family had, but I decided not to mention it aloud in case I jinxed it somehow.

"Your mum told you my family was involved with the hunters," I said. "Didn't she? She told you they were criminals and that my dad was a fairy."

"Among other things," she said. "She never liked your mother. But she didn't say much about your dad or why they jailed him. I tried to find out more, but the hunters keep that information under wraps."

"I didn't know you tried to learn more."

"Sure," she said. "Why wouldn't I? It's my history, too. Anyway, I'll see you around."

Before I could formulate a coherent response, she walked away, through the doors and out of the building.

Since when was Blythe remotely interested in why my dad had been arrested? Did she think he'd been arrested unjustly, too? I didn't think Blythe of all people would risk her neck on my behalf, but apparently, she had no intention of offering me an explanation. Not yet, anyway.

A chittering noise drew my attention to the corner of the lobby. The pixie crouched at the foot of the stairs, and one of his wings was bent sideways.

"Hey." I hurried over to him. "Are you okay?"

Had the police caught him in Blythe's house? Wait—no, the elves had spoken to him in the forest afterwards. He was the one who'd told them the Pixie-Glass was with Nathan's family. Nathan's dad hadn't hurt him, had he?

I knelt down at his side, seeing that he clutched a letter in his hands. My heart skipped a beat as I gently tugged it from his hands.

Then I saw the words on the paper, and my blood iced over.

Blair Wilkes. I heard about your involvement in current events. Have you rethought your decision to turn down my offer of employment?

The Inquisitor.

He'd sent me a message. He still wanted to recruit me.

"Blair?" said a voice from behind me. "What is that?"

I rose to my feet, my heart lurching in my chest. "Madame Grey."

The leading witch approached me, one eye on the pixie, the other on the note in my hand. Busted.

"Is that pixie with you?" she enquired.

"No, but he's hurt, and it's my fault." My thoughts were spinning in circles. "I'm sorry. I should have told you. The Inquisitor still wants me to join the hunters. And he knows... he knows I'm a fairy because he is one." The words came out in a rush. "Did you know?"

She shook her head. "No, but this answers a lot of questions I've had ever since his visit. Let me see this message of his."

I showed her the note, and she leaned over to read it, her glasses perched on the end of her nose.

I swallowed hard. "I think he hurt the pixie to get at me. But I never—I mean, I turned down his offer the last time he tried to recruit me. I didn't know he was a fairy at the time, but now... he knows I know. He'll come here."

"I see," said Madame Grey.

"And?" My body tensed. This was it. The threat to Fairy Falls was too much, and now she was going to tell me to leave.

"If he wants to make an open challenge to us, then let him come," she said. "Let them come."

My mouth fell open. "What? Seriously? You want them to come here?"

"I hoped the Inquisitor and his ilk would stay away, but it seems they have other ideas." Her expression was pure steel. "But I will not let them recruit any of my witches. If they threaten anyone here in Fairy Falls, then we will be ready for them."

Resolve strengthened me. We'd face the hunters, head-on, no matter what happened. I'd find a way to contact my dad, and if the hunters came here again?

Fairy Falls would be ready.

ABOUT THE AUTHOR

Elle Adams lives in the middle of England, where she spends most of her time reading an ever-growing mountain of books, planning her next adventure, or writing. Elle's books are humorous mysteries with a paranormal twist, packed with magical mayhem.

She also writes urban and contemporary fantasy novels as Emma L. Adams.

Find Elle on Facebook at https://www.facebook.com/pg/ElleAdamsAuthor/